"Wha... with This Door?"

He rattled the knob, but the door refused to yield.

"It's locked."

"I see. Unlock it," he rapped out in command, "or I'll smash it in. You have five seconds to weigh the odds."

At the count of five he stood looking down at her flushed face. His pallor, beneath his tan, took her breath away and made it difficult to swallow.

"Don't ever again try to bar me from your room, Petrina. From your room — or from your bed!"

Dear Reader,

Silhouette Romances is an exciting new publishing series, dedicated to bringing you the very best in contemporary romantic fiction from the very finest writers. Our stories and our heroines will give you all you want from romantic fiction.

Also, *you* play an important part in our future plans for Silhouette Romances. We welcome any suggestions or comments on our books, which should be sent to the address below.

So enjoy this book and all the wonderful romances from Silhouette. They're for *you*.

Silhouette Books
Editorial Office
47 Bedford Square
LONDON
WC1B 3DP

DOROTHY VERNON
Kissed by Moonlight

Silhouette Romance

Published by Silhouette Books

Copyright © 1981 by Dorothy Vernon

First printing 1981

British Library C.I.P.

Vernon, Dorothy
  Kissed by moonlight.
  I. Title
  823'.914   PR6072.E75

SBN 0-340-27114-0

Printed and bound in Canada for
Hodder and Stoughton Paperbacks, a
division of Hodder and Stoughton Ltd.,
Mill Road, Dunton Green, Sevenoaks,
Kent (Editorial Office: 47 Bedford
Square, London, WC1 3DP)

Kissed by Moonlight

Chapter One

Petrina's face was pressed into the pillow that was acting as a sponge for her tears, which was why she didn't hear the man climbing in through her bedroom window. She first saw her midnight intruder as a shadow, dramatically elongated, on the white wall.

She knew immediately it was the press; it was always the press these days. "Why won't you leave me alone?" It was a plea.

She reached out a hand, meaning to switch on her bedside lamp. Impulse intervened, as it so often did because she was a woman given to spontaneous action. Instead, she threw the table lamp at him.

He ducked. The lamp crashed against the wall; her bed sank silently under his extra weight. She shivered in horror. Fear, plus the proximity of his long, supple strength, acted as a momentary silencer. Before she had the wit to scream, his hand clamped down on her mouth. She bit it.

"You little vixen. I'm here to—"

"Get off my bed. This is unpardonable—"

"For heaven's sake, list—"

"—trespass," she yelled at him.

She would have said more, but his mouth closed on hers; no doubt he thought that would shut her up. She hit out at him, trying desperately to regain her freedom.

"All right, if that's how you want it." His laugh grated on her senses, tapping a memory that was slow to form.

The kiss deepened, and suddenly she knew who he was. Her first guess that he was one of the newspaper reporters who'd hounded her for days, going to diabolical lengths to interview her, was wrong. Even the most unscrupulous of them wouldn't resort to this.

"You're not the press," she hissed at him.

"Of course I'm not. A couple of characters who look as if they might be are lurking outside. That's why I decided to come in this way instead of using the door."

"What do you want of me?" she demanded.

"I thought *you* might want something of *me.*"

Three years ago when they last met, yes. Not now.

"Go to the devil," she spat at him in fiery indignation. Then she thought again, and added, "What did you think I might want?"

"Protection."

"Thank you, but I can look after myself," she replied with a return of spirit.

His low chuckle went part way to agreeing with her bold statement. "A while ago I might have argued with that. Now I'm inclined to believe you. For a lightweight, you've got quite a punch, Petrina."

In the remote event of her needing to have her suspicions regarding his identity confirmed, his use of her unusual name would have been proof enough. David had always called her Petrina. To the press she was Trina Nightingale, and the majority of her friends called her Trina as well. If people thought about it at all, they generally assumed it to be a shortening of the name Katrina.

It was pure perversity that made her ask, "Am I supposed to know you?"

"Always the joker. Want me to put the light on so that you can see me?"

She would have said yes, but for the teasing note in his voice that gave her memory a nudge. Before crawling into bed she'd indulged in a temper tantrum, throwing her various possessions everywhere. It had been a stupid and pointless release, serving no useful purpose, and tomorrow she would have the ignoble task of picking everything up and restoring order. It wasn't the state of the room that bothered her, though. She didn't care a toss what he thought of that. Her concern was of a more personal nature. She'd thrown literally everything she could lay her hands on, including her nightgown, as his restraining hands could bear witness, hence the inflection in his voice.

She heard the groping noises as he reached for the quilt that had slithered to the floor. She felt its comforting bulk being wrapped around her. Only then did he switch on the light so that she could see his mocking face.

"Hello," she said resignedly to David Palmer, the son of her dearest and most trusted friend, Professor Richard Palmer.

Three years ago, when she was eighteen, she had imagined herself to be in love with the much older

David. She had extended her foolishness a step further by telling him so. A rebuff was the last thing she had expected. She had the looks; her father had the money. Who would turn down that irresistible combination? Who but David? He had callously informed her that she was a promising child. "Look me up in several years' time," he had drawled, "when they've let you out of school."

Her lip had trembled but she'd stood her ground. "I'm not a child. Girls aren't children at eighteen these days," she screamed at him. "You're a rat."

She would have pushed past him, but nobody called him a rat and got away with it. He'd held her by the wrists and forced her to come forward until she was directly under his chin. The tangy fresh smell of his after-shave—a blend of sage, laurel, and oak moss—had teased her nose until she was looking up at him. She had wrenched her wrists free, but mischief had prompted her to wind her hands up around his neck and clasp her fingers tightly together.

He had groaned and said, "The ring of seduction." She hadn't known what he meant and he didn't explain it to her.

" And don't ever say that to me," he'd added tersely. "Don't ever call me a rat again."

Her full child's mouth, colored by nature that soft shade of pink that beauticians aim in vain to create, had pouted at him as she sought to hide her pain. "I suppose understatement would bother you. You're not just any old rat. You're King Rat."

She'd looked scared then, as if it had just occurred to her that she'd gone too far. She didn't know that the signs she was reading—the swift shallow breathing, the dilated pupils—were due to arousal. Half-child that she had been, she was gullible enough to believe him when he said he had no interest in her.

"I'm not King Rat. That title deservedly belongs to your father."

She kept right on looking at him with her huge, reproachful eyes, biting heavily on her lip. She couldn't know that he'd retaliated in anger because of his own response to her nearness.

Regret had washed over his features. "I didn't mean that, and whether I meant it or not is immaterial. I shouldn't have said it. I'm sorry. Sorry for my quick tongue. Sorry for the things you have yet to find out."

She'd found them out the next day. It was three years ago and still the pain of remembering hurt. No wonder he hadn't wanted anything to do with her. Her father was no longer a highly respected man of great wealth and power. The words the press bandied about—fraudulent transactions, currency infringements, secretive deals, financial failure, tax investigations—spelled out the crash of his vast business empire.

In the nightmare days that followed there was a lot that was not entirely clear to her. Her father had started modestly with little more than a wild brilliance and the ambition to back it up. Wherever his Midas hand touched he brought jobs and prosperity. Perhaps he never realized he'd succeeded in what he'd set out to do. Perhaps he found it too stultifying to sit back and lord it in luxury. Restless ambition stirred his brain. He dreamed of having an interest in an island sunspot—a small, neglected chunk of land that was waiting to be reclaimed and turned into a holiday paradise. Nothing trashy or commercialized, though. Just white villas, a few select shops. A hotel, even two, tastefully secluded in a green and fragrant setting of pine. Sickle-shaped beaches, peace, relaxation—everything his overworked brain and body craved for when he planned a holiday. The island of Chimera.

He made his first error ever, the error of looking at the scheme with too personal an eye. He'd always known intuitively what the public wanted and he had given it to them irrespective of whether it coincided with his own taste. Perhaps he'd stumbled on the formula of success by accident and wasn't aware of it. This time he was going to give the public what *he* wanted, whether *they* wanted it or not.

He advertised both at home and abroad for parties interested in taking out a concession in the venture. The response was enormous. King Midas, as he was affectionately called, couldn't fail, and people from all walks of life wanted a stake in any project that carried the charisma of his name.

From the beginning there were snags. One was the tight control on sterling movement. Permission was rarely given for the transfer of the amount he envisaged without a cast-iron guarantee of a quick return of foreign capital.

He got his plan off the ground, but there were too many things against him. The unprecedented rise in aviation charges brought on by the severe energy crisis was only one of many hurdles to be overcome. Several of the investors pulled out when they saw how things were going and this show of lost confidence moved others to do the same. The final blow came when the package tour operators weren't enthusiastic and declined to include his resort in their holiday brochures. Their support had been vital, but as far as they were concerned the very things that Benjamin Nightingale had pressed for—the peace and quiet and exquisite natural beauty of an unspoiled location—proved its downfall. It wasn't commercial enough, they said.

The dream had shattered at his feet. Benjamin Nightingale not only lost his Midas touch, but almost his mind, as the full weight of the disaster hit him. He escaped going to prison because someone stepped in to buy him out. He dodged the abuse and the condemnation of the same public who had hoisted him up onto his golden throne by fleeing to a secret hideaway in Scotland. The press had a field day, latching predictably on to such headlines as "The King Has Fallen" or, another favorite, "The Bird Has Flown."

Petrina had begged her father to take her with him, but he had refused all entreaty. It hurt that he did not want her by his side but she understood that he was driven almost by instinct. In the way that a hurt animal drags himself to his lair to lick his wounds in private, so he wanted some time alone.

Although her mother had died many years before, Petrina was lucky to have a staunch protector in Professor Richard Palmer, a widower like her father and her father's friend. He took her into his home and persuaded her to continue with her schooling. Before her father's financial crash, her name had been put down for her to go to an exclusive school in the south of England. As far as she was concerned, that was now out of the question.

"But Uncle Richard," she had argued, "there's no money to pay for it." The "uncle" was a courtesy title only, honoring his long-standing family friendship.

"It's been set aside for you."

"My father lost everything. He couldn't have made provision for my education."

"Who mentioned your father?"

"Then who?"

13

He had given a small embarrassed laugh. "Sometimes it's better not to ask these things, my child."

But she knew who her kind benefactor was. Uncle Richard himself.

"I can't take your savings."

"I'd insist that you did, if I had any. I'm not the financial genius in this family, though," he'd said, a wicked reminder that it was his son, David, who was that and more. "I've nothing to speak of in the bank and I have to draw on my own resources. I'm as rich as my next salary check." The grin on his face had slid into a look of genuine concern. "I would have been happy to pay your school fees, even at some sacrifice, but it was never asked of me."

She hadn't believed him. She had reached up to kiss his cheek, for his generosity and for his modesty in telling a white lie so that he would not be embarrassed by her thanks.

She had settled down reasonably well at school. Her father had been less content in Scotland, in his whitewashed crofter's cottage. He soon tired of the heather-and bracken-clad banks and braes. The windy spaces, this bonny refuge, could no longer appease his exiled heart. His restless thoughts migrated to the city streets of his birthplace. He had to make a comeback. He reasoned it out in his mind that he'd gone into the holiday project with insufficient knowledge. He wouldn't make that mistake again. He hit upon a plan, bolder than the first one, but still, he was convinced, within his capabilities. He had the flair and determination to succeed, and also the knowledge. What he didn't have was the money; he needed a stake. There must still have been some charisma attached to his name because he got it. The speculators readily came in, and he was in harness again. Petrina joined him; she left school to keep house for him.

Why he failed this second time was beyond comprehension. Perhaps it was because the first failure had killed the dash of recklessness that bold plans need to succeed. Whatever the reason, two years and eleven months after the first crash his second venture failed, leaving him a bitterly disillusioned, defeated man.

All the dirt of the earlier project was raked up by the press. It barely concerned him because this time his health as well as his spirit broke. He knew he could not make another comeback. He was finished. He had nothing to live for, and he gave up living.

The press, true to form right to the end, hinted that in a moment of abject depression he had taken his own life. In her grief, it was one small consolation to Petrina that the coroner's report showed he died of natural causes.

At the funeral there was no lack of spectators; the morbid curiosity seekers were there in abundance. But only two real mourners were present—Petrina and her dear, steadfast friend, the man who had been like another father to her, Professor Richard Palmer.

Afterward, in the quiet pub where she was picking at her food in an attempt to please the professor because she knew how worried he was about her, he said, "I sent a wire to David. I thought he might have made it here in time to pay his last respects."

She hadn't set eyes on his son for close to three years, not since the eve of her father's first crash when she had impulsively blurted out her love for him. She would have been surprised to see David Palmer paying something to her father in death that he hadn't felt for him in life. He might have respected him when he was doing well, but he had no respect for a failure. And no thought for anyone who just happened to be caught in the backwash of that failure.

The professor, who had a knack for coming out with things to make life easier to understand, had once likened life to a lake. You cast in your lot and make a ripple. It can be a peaceful ripple or a gigantic splash.

Now she said, "My father made a maelstrom in the lake of life and drowned in it, didn't he?"

"Yes," he said, sighing deeply. "We should remember that we are not the only ones in the lake. The turbulence we make spreads out to affect others. Those closest are the worst affected. It will still after a while, Trina." He patted her hand and said briskly, "If you've quite finished pushing that food about your plate, I'm going to take you home with me."

She was glad to be released from the burden of pretense and willingly abandoned her knife and fork for her coat. But once outside the pub, walking with her hand thrust companionably in the crook of his arm, she said, "Thank you, it's kind of you and I appreciate it, but I can't come home with you. I must go back to the flat."

"You said *must,* not *want,*" he observed shrewdly.

"I can't explain it," she said.

"Some things don't need explaining. You are your father's daughter; you'll never pick the easy fences."

She felt ashamed. She wasn't being noble or brave in wanting to face up to life by herself, if that was what he thought. Yet there was some truth in his words. She *was* her father's daughter, and as in her father, the instinct to crawl back to her lair and lick her wounds in solitude went deep.

But the solitude she craved was not to be found. To get through the door she had to fight her way past a barrage of the same reporters who had tormented her for days. She didn't know why they thought she was hot news, why they wanted to pick over the dead bones.

She came up out of her thoughts to anchor the quilt more firmly about her body. "It's been a long time, David."

"Long enough to sink past grievances, wouldn't you say?"

Only he would purposely bring back the memory of their last meeting when she'd thrown herself at him. That sort of cruelty was only what she expected of him, yet it still made her draw her breath in sharply.

"I made a fool of myself. I'm older now, and it won't happen again."

"Pity. I wouldn't mind it happening now."

She gritted her teeth. "Look, you've frightened the life out of me by bouncing in like this. Would you mind telling me what you want and then leaving?"

His handsome face wore a pained expression. "I've already explained my unorthodox entrance. I didn't want to run the gauntlet of the press at your expense. It wouldn't do your image any good to have reports of a gentleman caller at this hour of night. Not so soon after . . ." His voice trailed off.

"Get on with it," she said, not wanting to fall into the trap of saying, "Where's the gentleman?" knowing full well that a fitting answer to that would be waiting to trip off his lips. Now she came to think about it she'd always resented his ability to think faster than normal people. That trait, combined with a certain subtlety of wit, had given her many uncomfortable moments in the past.

"I'm offering you the means to escape the harassment of the press."

"What means? And what's in it for you, David? You

never offer anything unless you're assured of a good return."

His indrawn breath was as audible as the narrowing of his eyelids was noticeable.

"You don't like being reminded of how ruthless you are, do you, David?"

"I prefer the word *astute.*"

"Of course you would."

Successful in all business undertakings, he seemed to run on a never-ending electric current, but she knew the real power behind him was ambition. She was frightened of ambition. Look what it had done to her father. He, too, had pursued success with grim determination, but it had turned around to snap back at him and had hounded him into his grave.

"Don't you think I'm capable of doing a kindness without having an ulterior motive?"

"It would be most unlikely."

"Perhaps you're right," he drawled. "Even supposedly kind people only do good deeds because they think they're securing a place in heaven for themselves."

"That sounds more like the David I remember."

"You're not like the Petrina I remember, though. You've changed. The promise was always there, but I didn't realize you'd grow into such a riveting beauty."

He moved from his sitting position on the edge of the bed and stood up. He towered over her. Her jawline went rigid; she threw her head tautly back to look up at him, as though she dare not let him slip the net of her gaze.

His bright blue eyes were knowing, derisive, and full of rebuke. "All the changes aren't for the better. You've grown cynical and suspicious. I liked the gullible child best."

His patronizing tone irked her. Her soft brown-violet

eyes took on the harsher color of smoke. With assumed arrogance, as though she were acting on someone else's orders, she said, in reckless mimicry of his own derision, "You had your chance with her. You didn't take it."

"No, I didn't." His blue eyes were as piercing as a dagger. As she managed the strength not to look away, she thought she saw a flicker of something—regret, nostalgia, longing—shadow his gaze, but it was just as quickly swept away. His face was composed as he said, "You do some things in life that put others out of reach."

She felt she should remember those words. Somewhere there was a clue that was begging to be recognized.

He added, in a low voice that was like the release of an inner thought, "You don't know how close a thing it was, though."

For a tantalizing moment she almost believed that her yesterday self, that gauche child, had touched some nerve of awareness in this experienced, wordly man. It was a beautiful, incandescent thought, but even as she held it so briefly it burned her so she had to let it go. The evidence of it remained as two dots of color in her cheeks.

"Will you please stop playing with me," she cried out in anguish.

With the slip of her control, his was regained, almost as if the one was dependent on the other. It was a pattern that had been set long ago, for their relationship had never been an easy one. If one showed normal kindness or betrayed tenderness, the other met it with scorn and ridicule.

"Playing with you?" he mocked, with enough undercurrents in his tone to keep her cheeks rosy with embarrassment. "What an intriguing picture that con-jures up."

"You must work hard to be this hateful," she said. "Such a polished performance can only come with hours of practice." She swung her feet over the edge of the bed. "If you won't get out of here, then I will. I'd rather battle it out with the reporters than stomach you for a moment longer."

"Poor little Petrina," he taunted, with laughter in his eyes. "I always did get under your skin. Incidentally, dignity in dishabille is impossible to achieve. Why don't you—" He was obviously looking around for some garment to hand to her that was more fitting than the quilt, and for the first time he took in the disorder of the room. "Good heavens! Are you al-ways this untidy?"

"Of course not. I had a throwing session, a tantrum, an indulgence you would never permit yourself."

"No, I can't see the profit in it," he said in mild amusement, as though he knew he was offering her bait that she would find impossible to resist.

"The *profit!*" she scoffed before she realized she had been manipulated to say just that. "I hate you, David Palmer. Hate you . . . hate . . ."

"Not tears," he said in disgust on seeing the liquid sparkle in her eyes.

She could have said, "Why not tears? After all, I'm grieving for my father," but she would not beg for his sympathy. So she bit savagely on her lower lip until the pain blanched it white and she'd recovered from her lapse into self-pity.

"If I were as inhuman as you care to believe, I wouldn't be here at all," he said gravely.

"Why *are* you here?" Although she spat the words at

him, her eyes were curious. After all, he still hadn't told her how he could help her, as he had apparently come to do.

His regard was thoughtful. "Before I answer that, have you made any plans?"

In a threadlike voice that matched her lowered head, she said, "No, I've still to decide what to do." She was instantly ashamed of that hint of fatigue, of her despairing weariness, and visibly lifted herself up by her chin, which again pointed at him in defiance. "Strange as it may seem to you, I've needed all my resources to get through the last few days."

His nod of agreement confounded her. It was that, and not the prospect facing her, that put a wobble in her voice. "I shall have to get a job."

"That does sound drastic," he observed in cool amusement. "You're not considering selling your life story to the press? Obviously that's why you're being persecuted by that battery of reporters. On the further assumption that each one is battling for exclusive rights, you could earn yourself a tidy sum."

"Even you wouldn't insult me by thinking that I might be tempted to accept, no matter how much money I was offered," she said, devouring him in anger with her eyes.

"People do all manner of things when they're in a corner."

His contrasting cool sent her temper flaring even higher. "And you think I'm in a corner?"

"Aren't you? How do you intend to set about earning your living? What did that expensive school equip you to do?"

In truth, she was forced to reply, "Very little, beyond putting on the social airs and graces. It was my father's

21

choice, not mine. And when he made it he couldn't have foreseen a time when I'd need to earn my own living. I left as soon as I could."

"To stay at home, I understand. You didn't go out and get a job."

"Do you think I didn't want to? Somebody had to keep house for my father. I'd have been a lot happier training to do something useful. Perhaps it isn't too late now, as soon as the dust has settled. I don't fancy the notoriety of being pointed out as the daughter of a fallen idol. That's in case you think I'm employing delaying tactics, putting off the evil day."

"I don't blame you for wanting to lie low until it's all blown over, but I won't stand by and see you climbing on my father's back to do it."

"What do you mean by that?"

His dark eyebrows went up in mild surprise that she needed it spelled out. "He hasn't the financial strength to give you a piggyback ride."

She chewed on her lip. "Did you know that your father has offered me a home?"

"I didn't, but I guessed he might have done. He's very fond of you."

"It's not a one-way thing. I'm fond of him. I'm already too indebted to him, though. I won't sponge off him any longer than necessary, if that's what's bothering you."

"It doesn't seem to bother *you*."

The challenge bewildered her, but she answered truthfully, "No, because he knows that if the position was reversed, he could rely on me for help."

"That's true. But would he let you help him? He's a proud, stubborn man. I wanted to make up his losses three years ago, but he wouldn't hear of it."

She felt that he'd said more about his father's plight

than he had meant to. Her opinion of David, the man, might be unfavorable, but she knew that he loved his father and that no man could have been a more devoted son. He'd fallen into the very human trap of being carried away by his own frustration because he wasn't allowed to help. She didn't want to believe what David seemed to hinting. After all, his brilliant brain and business acumen had rocketed him into an income bracket that must make his father's modest earnings seem like a pittance in comparison. At the same time, she found herself giving David a long, thoughtful look.

"You said your father suffered a financial loss three years ago?" Her eyes traced the dark contours of his face, sliding along the powerful jawline to the uncompromising straightness of his mouth.

"Yes," he said grudgingly.

Her head shifted to a speculative angle. "That would be around the time of my father's first failure, when his plan to turn Chimera into a holiday haven crashed. A lot of small investors lost their entire savings." A chill touched her heart. "Was your father one of them?"

He was on his guard now, and intended to stay tight-lipped on the subject.

She sighed in resignation. "I know from past experience that if you've made up your mind not to tell me, nothing I can say will make you. But you don't have to say anything. Your silence has said it all for you."

She looked down at her fingers in sad thought. She was sorry for those who had invested in good faith and lost their money; it grieved her to think that anyone with that sort of trust in her father's abilities should lose by it. It was especially hurtful to know that dear Uncle Richard had been a victim. He would have been too loyal to pull out when so many others had.

She was aware of David's eyes narrowing on her hair.

It was the color of pale copper with burnished high-lights, and she was suddenly conscious of the tangling her pillow-pounding had achieved. She wished she'd had time to brush it into shiny obedience.

She wasn't coy about her looks. She liked her neck, which was long and slender, a beautiful asset. But she disliked her cheeks, which were still roundly cushioned from childhood; likewise her mouth was full, but she didn't mind that at all. She had good legs, quite long in proportion to her body, which she wished she'd had time to drape in something a little more seductive than this stupid quilt.

The wishing coincided with a sudden alarming aware-ness of David's good looks. He was tall, leanly built but muscular, with the brightest blue eyes she had ever seen in a strong, suntanned face. His dark hair was crisp, undisciplined, and full of natural vigor. Like the man himself.

Would it have made any difference if his first peep at her hadn't been over the pink frills of her crib? He would have been twelve at the time. Would she ever catch up on those twelve years? And if they'd met now for the first time, with no memories of the slippery pink infant naked in her bath or the tiresome child who wanted to tag along, would he see her in a different light?

Her mouth rounded on a small despairing sigh. Even if she "accidentally on purpose" let the quilt slip, his mind's eye would still see the slippery pink infant and not the woman she was.

She drew a long, hard breath and would have linked her hands together for courage, but she needed them to clutch the quilt more tightly around her. Too much had happened in too short a time. Her father's sudden death, his funeral, the hammering she was taking from the press, David's unexpected reappearance, and the knowledge that Uncle Richard had lost money in her father's failed venture. She couldn't take much more; she was nearly over the top.

"All right, David, you've stalled long enough. Just what is the nature of this escape line you are offering me?"

"It's in the nature of a proposal. I'm asking you to marry me."

"You can't be. It's too unthinkable."

"The idea of marriage? Or being married to me?" For once she was glad not to be granted the right of reply as he went on to say, "I see I've shocked you. It would shock my father a great deal more if I carried you off without marrying you."

"But, Dav—"

"It's all arranged. Pack for a warm climate. Don't bother about the flat. I'll leave instructions for it to be disposed of together with the furniture and whatever possessions you can't take. Anything you can't bear to part with, my father will store for you. The wedding will take place tomorrow; by evening you'll be far away from it all. Any questions?"

She was silent; she had no idea what to say, how to react.

"Good. Get some sleep now, you need it. I'll be back for you tomorrow, around noon."

When he'd gone she climbed wearily back into bed. Her whole life had been turned upside down, but one thing remained constant. Her feeling for David had not changed. She could wish him at the edge of the earth for his overbearing manner and his supreme arrogance, but she still loved him.

Chapter Two

She wondered why she'd assumed that because it was all arranged in a hurry the ceremony would take place in a registry office and not in a church.

David came for her at midday, having badgered the authorities to obtain a special license and the services of a vicar, and pulled strings to get flight reservations in between giving orders for the flat and any remaining possessions to be disposed of so that she could walk out and start new. He'd even remembered to buy the ring.

"I must be insane to be going through with this," she said, taking two steps to his one to keep up with his long stride. "I'm not sure that I will go through with it. Why are you doing this, David?"

"Don't you know?" he inquired, his smile as evasive as his reply.

"Would I ask if I did? In my present circumstances

I'm hardly value for money. What's in it for you? What's your angle?"

"Would you like it better if I had one?"

"I don't know about that. It would make more sense."

"Very well, I admit it. I've got an angle."

She waited expectantly, but he didn't elaborate. She sent him a soft sideways look through her lashes, which she knew would avail her nothing. "You're not going to tell me, are you?"

"No." He softened sufficiently to add—or was it not softening at all but blatant teasing?—"I might tell you someday. If I decide you deserve to be told."

"You're an arrogant beast," she said.

He only grinned sardonically in reply.

"It doesn't seem real," she protested. "I can't believe this is my wedding day."

"Like a dream?"

Her tongue flicked up to lick her lip in an unconsciously provocative way. "Nightmare, actually."

She thought he looked very smart. He wore a quiet gray suit and a darker gray silk tie and a remarkable air of assurance.

She wondered if her own hurried choice of dress was appropriate. It couldn't be the white wedding gown she'd always hoped to get married in, but she had gone for chastity in a simple parchment-colored day dress, leaving her arms bare but her throat demurely covered in a close-fitting bodice.

Uncle Richard was waiting for them on the steps of the church. "Will you honor my arm on the walk down the aisle, my child?" he asked in a voice that was choked with emotion and delight. Apparently he had been thrilled by news of the impending wedding and had chosen not to ask any potentially embarrassing questions.

"Indeed I will," she said, reaching up to kiss his dear cheek.

David had already entered the church, presumably to alert the vicar, so they had these few private moments alone.

"I know about the money," she said.

"How did you find out? David didn't tell you."

"Only very indirectly. I guessed."

He sighed heavily. "In a way I'm glad you know. It was David's own idea to accept responsibility for you. I would have paid your school fees, but, well, I made a bad investment."

"Uncle Richard, it's the bad investment I'm talking about."

"You didn't know about—"

"No. I didn't know it was David who paid my school fees."

"Seems I've blown it, haven't I?"

"Yes, Uncle Richard."

"Don't let on to David, will you?"

"No, I promise not to give you away. I won't be long," she said, detaching herself from his impulsive hug. "There's something . . ."

She saw from his expression that he thought she'd changed her mind and was running away, so she made pantomime actions to indicate it wasn't that. She thought he understood as she wriggled through the gap in the church wall and plunged into the tall grass of the field beyond.

Her fingers searched for the abundance of flowers she knew she would find and soon she had a wedding bouquet of buttercups and bluebells, honeysuckle and toadflax, columbines, oxeye daisies, and other field flowers. She secured her sweet-smelling posy in a border of wild pansies and tied them up with her handkerchief. Then she searched around for two wild roses, sparing the time to find perfect specimens. A bride had to have a bouquet, her bridegroom and his father had to have boutonnieres. Why, oh, why did it have to be David who had paid her school fees?

Without choir, organ, or congregation, she walked down the aisle on her future father-in-law's arm in the vast but beautiful emptiness of the gray stone church toward her bridegroom.

She knew why brides wore full veils over their faces. It was to conceal such emotions as she was feeling now. Yet the half-light was kindly. What it couldn't veil was the trembling of her fingers in the crook of the professor's arm as he whispered hoarsely, "I wish your mother could have been here to see you. And your father."

Perhaps they were. Were those wooden pews totally empty? Did gentle images cluster in the darkest corners? Was it silence ringing in her ears or the faint echo of a celestial choir?

A spear of sunshine shafting down from a stained-glass window touched them with its rosy glow. It was like a benediction.

She squeezed the professor's arm and whispered, "Dear Uncle Richard."

And then she was conscious of David's solemn face above her. He looked almost tender, as if he cared that she was to become his wife. She shook her head, as if to remove the image. To imagine that David was moved was taking fantasy too far.

The ring that David had placed on her finger now glinted in the bright sunshine as she held it out for the professor's inspection. Her hand was taken into the comforting custody of his larger one. "Truly my daughter at last," he said, humbling her beyond speech.

David said, in an odd, clipped voice, as though scoffing at the childishness that had prompted the action, "When I saw the posy of wild flowers, I half expected you to come to me barefoot."

"I almost did." She looked down at the soaked toes of her ruined shoes. "These weren't manufactured with tramps through long, wet grass in mind."

Because David's censorious, mocking eyes were upon her, she dared not steal a flower to be sentimentally pressed in a treasured book, so she handed her wild-flower wedding bouquet intact to the first little girl they passed.

The professor still proudly wore his sweet-scented dog rose, but David's lapel was bare of adornment. His boutonniere had been conveniently lost, it would seem.

A jet took them on the first stage of their journey. She didn't know where David was taking her. He hadn't volunteered the information and she hadn't asked. In any case, the moment they were airborne he'd unzipped some papers from his brief case, prohibiting conversation.

He had apologized before starting work on them. "I'm sorry about this, but it's got to be done today. If I must neglect you sometime, better now than later. It wouldn't do to burn the midnight oil on our wedding night."

Her eyelids dropped, weighted by a great shyness. As his eyes traveled down the papers on his knee, ticking a figure here, heavily scoring out another there, the implication of his words shredded her composure. The haste had been for her convenience—she had needed to get away quickly—but it was clear that it was not going to be a marriage of convenience for him too. Only David would take it for granted that the marriage would be consummated without bothering about the cosseting ritual of courtship. It was going to be very strange. Although she had known him all her life, nurturing a secret passion for him for most of that time, she had never tingled in his arms or gently rebuffed the probings of his hands in their attempt to know her body. Yet tonight he would take it as his right to know her intimately.

The jet touched down at a large airport and she found herself boarding another plane, one that was much smaller.

"Not the last thing in comfort, but it'll do for the short time we'll be on it," David said in token apology. "The runway of the airport we're making for is being extended to take jets. It should be operational by the end of the year."

He seemed to be telling her something, but she wasn't intuitive enough to know what. She smiled and said vaguely, "Oh, really!" Just as though he was making inconsequential chatter, which was something he never did.

When he said, "We're almost there now," she looked down at an amazingly blue sea, angling her head to get a better view of a collection of islands.

The smallest island of all was set a little apart from its sister group. It had a curious outline; its rugged coastline wound in and out in a series of animal shapes. The most distinctive animal shape of all was at its southern tip, and it was like no animal she had known. Tracing its shape she saw that it almost had a lion's head, a goat's body, and it flicked off into a serpent's tail.

Suddenly she knew where David was taking her. She found herself speaking its name, although she had never set eyes on it before. "Chimera." Her throat was tight with emotion. This moment would live forever in her heart, her first sight of Chimera. "It's my father's island. It's Chimera!"

The dream that went amiss. The venture of three years ago that had toppled his empire and started the avalanche that had brought about his ruin. Yet it was not that aspect she thought about as she gazed down at Chimera with tears in her eyes.

"I've always wanted to tread my father's dream. It's the perfect honeymoon surprise. Thank you for bringing me here, David. You can't know how much I appreciate your thoughtfulness."

Even before he answered, by looking at his face she knew her gratitude was misplaced.

He demanded crossly, "Just when did you think I had time to make extravagant honeymoon plans?"

He was right. There had been no time for him to arrange a honeymoon; no time for her to shop for her trousseau. Her mouth curved at the thought that perhaps her old cotton nightgown was just the job for a nonhoneymoon.

"It's simply an unkind coincidence that I have to bring you to the place of that ill-fated venture of your father's. It's where I happen to be working at the moment. I'm with the hotel."

"How stupid of me," she said stiffly.

"It's no good taking that attitude, Petrina. My father seemed to think you needed my support and he was right. I'm glad he sent for me, but the fact remains that I had to leave several important things hanging fire that I must go back and attend to."

"I hope you won't find my presence an encumbrance,

and I am not taking any attitude," she said, warding off that weak feminine reaction to cruelty.

She was deeply disappointed that she was tagging along with him and that he had not planned to bring her here to please her, even though she knew that because of the time factor, and because he didn't really care for her at all, she was being unreasonable. It was cruel of him not to let her cling to her father's dream and instead make her face up to the reality that it had brought about his destruction. Why was he doing this to her? Why was he being so unkind?

It didn't occur to her that he might be trying to prepare her for something, not even when he said, "I'm truly sorry, Petrina," as if this was just the beginning of the disillusionment in store for her.

She would not let him spoil it for her. Despite his chilling words, she felt a strange tingle of excitement at the prospect of seeing Chimera for herself. Chimera— by its very name standing for illusion and enchantment, not disillusion and disenchantment—would surely make her dreams come true, not destroy them.

In a marginally kinder voice he said, "If I sound brusque it might be because I feel inadequate. To a man it doesn't matter." His penetrating gaze increased her discomfort. "I should have realized that certain things are important to a woman, and a honeymoon is certainly one of them. I've cheated you. I should never have brought you to Chimera."

No, no, he was wrong. It was destined for him to bring her here.

"Poor Pet-rina." The break in her name was deliberate, because then he said, "My poor little Pet." He could almost have said "my poor little darling," or even "my poor little love," because he used the shortening of her name in a way that no one had done before, as an endearment. "The trappings don't matter to me, but you should have had all the icing on the cake: a beautiful gown, a special bouquet and not a handful of wild flowers, bridesmaids galore, guests showering you with confetti and good wishes. Never mind the icing, you didn't even have the cake."

The plane gave a spine-jarring kangaroo hop and shuddered to a stop.

"Oh!" she exclaimed in some surprise, because she had been so absorbed in this talk with David that she hadn't realized what was happening. "We seem to have landed," she said with an air of disappointment. She was enjoying his kindness and would have liked the moment to be prolonged. He had been acting almost like a real bridegroom, a bridegroom who loved his bride.

The last remnants of color were draining from the day as she got into the car that was waiting for them. The porter who carried the cases welcomed David back with friendly deference, while his dark eyes floated a smile at Petrina.

The cases were in the trunk, the tip was in the man's hand, and David was at the wheel of the car preparing to drive off before he volunteered, "By the way, Manuel, this is my wife."

The man seemed speechless with surprise.

The light wasn't good enough for Petrina to see much of Chimera. They passed through the principal town, which David told her was called El Pueblo, The Town. It was comprised of a collection of whitewashed houses in a honeycomb of narrow cobbled streets that all ran into a tiny plaza dominated by a pretty little church.

"Three years ago the island was populated by old people," David informed her. "The young ones had all left for better opportunities, and who could blame them? Poverty makes for exploitation. They saw their fathers and grandfathers breaking their backs working the land with outdated methods and poor tools, while their mothers and grandmothers ruined their eyesight crocheting fine lace wear, tablecloths, and shawls, which they sold for a pittance. It used to be a sweatshop island, but thankfully all that has changed. The young men have come back to build the roads, the shops, and the hotels. The women returned to be with the men and, incidentally, to work in the shops and the hotels."

"You're very loyal, David."

"How do you mean? To whom am I loyal?"

"The opportunist who cashed in on my father's dream. I bet these poor people are still being exploited. Providing cheap labor."

"They're paid the going rate."

"Which I imagine would be unacceptable to any union back home," she said drily.

"This isn't England," he said, shrugging his shoulders and looking grim. "We're staying at the Hotel León, by the way. That's where I'm based."

"That sounds as though it should be situated on the lion's head," she said.

"Quite right, it is. I hope you don't hate it too much." Despite his solicitous words, his tone had gone indifferent again, as if it was just too bad if she did. In a kinder key he added, "I'll try to get things wound up quickly and then we'll go somewhere I think you *will* like."

On being escorted into the hotel, the surprised reaction that had flashed across the porter's face at the airport on being informed that she was David's wife was repeated several times over. It gave room for conjecture. It seemed that a straight eyebrow was maintained at the sight of a woman by his side, as if that was a familiar sight. The statement that she was his wife was the signal for a gasp of astonishment. Once again, she wondered what his angle had been, why he had taken a wife when he so obviously hadn't lacked for female company.

"Are you hungry?" he inquired.

"Yes, but I think I'm too exhausted to eat."

"Too exhausted to combat all the inquisitive eyes in the dining room, perhaps?" he asked intuitively.

"Yes, I do believe that's what I mean."

"Would you like to go straight up—" He smiled. "I was going to say to my suite, but it's our suite now. Yes? I'll collect the key and put you in the elevator, and I'll join you when I've seen if there's any mail and ordered a meal to be sent up."

"That sounds absolutely marvelous," she said, thankful he was not going to make her remain by his side, the object of so much astonishment and cool amusement.

She couldn't help teasing him about the way everyone was reacting to her presence. "Should you have sent prior warning that you were bringing a wife back with you? Have you put the cat among the pigeons?"

"Cat?" he mocked. "You're only a tiny defenseless kitten."

"Meow," she said, pulling a face at him.

He put her into the elevator and instructed the diminutive elevator boy, whose name she gathered was Ignacio, to escort her to their suite.

The lift whisked whisper-quiet to the top floor. She wondered what such a very large and pretentious hotel was doing on the premier site of her father's island. It should have been a much smaller establishment, sedate and dignified, to fit in with Chimera's unspoiled appeal.

Ignacio proudly conducted her to her door. *"Buenas noches, señora."*

"Buenas noches, Ignacio. *Gracias."* She knew very little Spanish, which was the language of the island, but saying goodnight and thank you was within her scope.

"De nada—it's nothing," he said, grinning as he went back to his post.

She inserted the key that David had given her into the lock, twisted it, and walked into a luxurious sitting room. David hadn't told her what he did at the hotel, but from the looks of this suite, she could tell that he was someone very important. Then her thoughts were broken as she noticed that the light was on. Odd. Probably the maid had been in recently and forgot to turn it off when she left. There was a desk in one corner, where David obviously worked, but it was primarily a room for relaxation with its deep, comfortable-looking armchairs, stereo unit, well-stocked bookshelves, and drinks cart. It was far from the impersonal hotel suite she had expected; David had made it into a home. There were two doors leading off—bedroom and bathroom? She left investigation of these for the time being and wandered out onto the balcony.

She couldn't see a thing out here because it was now quite dark, but she could hear the roll and tumble and swish of the sea. She rested her elbows on the balcony rail for a moment, staring out at nothing, soothed by the soft air and the blissful sound of the sea. It was obviously a small private balcony serving only this suite. Exploring further, she walked its length and found her way into the bedroom.

She came to an abrupt halt, gulping in shock. On one of the twin beds, reclining comfortably, was a woman in black silk lounging pajamas. Petrina judged her to be in

37

her early thirties. She had black hair wound into an immaculate chignon, ivory skin, and red-painted lips and fingernails.

The intruder rose up elegantly to view Petrina, implying in manner and by word that Petrina was the intruder. "On your way, sweetheart. I'm in residence."

"Your tenancy has just expired," Petrina informed her as coolly as she could, somehow managing to keep her head as all the pretty little dreams she had built, dreams of a David who would take her in his arms and tell her that he had loved her and missed her all these years, tumbled around her.

"Who do you think you are?" Miss Black Silk Pajamas inquired.

"David's wife," Petrina replied, her chin held desperately high. "*Mrs.* David Palmer."

A brittle laugh escaped the other's red mouth. "Top marks for inventive thinking. But David hasn't got a wife."

Petrina said, "I've had rather a hectic day, one way and another, and I'm very tired. Would you mind arguing it out with David. You'll find him down—"

"I don't need you to tell me where to find David," the woman said scornfully.

She located her shoes, taking a tormentingly long time to put them on, straining Petrina's nerves to the limit, but eventually she went. Petrina collapsed on the other bed, thoroughly shaken by the encounter.

What had she let herself in for? The hotel was too large, too garish, but she could hardly blame David for that. Apparently he just worked for the opportunist who had bought her father out. He probably hated the carousel atmosphere as much as she did. If he'd had time to plan things, he would undoubtedly have taken her somewhere very different for her bridal night. And of course David had sent her up to the suite all unsuspectingly. He could have had no idea that his lady friend would be waiting for him.

She must be reasonable about this. David was thirty-three and didn't give the impression of being a celibate. He had never tried to hide the fact that he liked women. He had a normal man's healthy outlook toward the opposite sex; his charm and good looks would insure that he was never without a companion to satisfy it.

How could she be reasonable? That bed, or its twin, was her bridal bed, and it was degrading to come up and find a woman on it, waiting for *her* lover.

By the time David joined her she had worked herself up into a state of anger that was so high and explosive that even he didn't possess enough charm and tact to calm her. Not, she supposed, that he would really care to make the effort anyway.

The cart bearing their supper arrived before David did. At first she thought it was David and she had sent the waiter a scalding look and had to bite back her angry words, which wasn't very bright of her. She could imagine him racing back down to the kitchen to tell his colleagues what a virago Señor Palmer had married.

David was smiling when he came in. "Not undressed yet? I would have thought that you couldn't wait to take a nice cool shower."

"And be all ready for you?" she taunted sweetly. "I didn't know that anyone had been in with the cases. I must have been in the bedroom when they arrived."

"The food's here, too," he observed. "Good. I'm ready for it." There was a perplexed frown on his face; he was obviously puzzled by her manner. "I'm sorry that I was longer than I said. Is that it? One thing led to another. You know how it is, Pet."

It had pleased her so much when he had called her Pet on the plane. Now it infuriated her. "No, I don't know how it is. But I'm beginning to suspect. And don't call me Pet. I'm neither your pet nor your plaything."

The brilliant blue eyes flicked over her; the puzzled frown remained as one dark eyebrow lifted. "Is this supposed to be a joke?" he asked in a voice that still managed, if only just, to maintain quiet reason.

"If it is, it's on me," she flung at him in fiery bitterness.

The eyebrow slammed down. He was not inquiring now, he was demanding. "What is this all about?"

"That's precisely what I'd like to know. What's it all about, David? Why *did* you marry me?"

But suddenly she knew why. She could read it in his eyes. He no longer regarded her as a child; moreover, she excited him as a woman.

He could hold a pause longer than she could. It was apparent that he was waiting for her to elaborate on what she'd said, and so she did. She was so steamed up she couldn't have kept her tongue still for another second.

"How silly of you to think of me in that way, David. The one woman you couldn't have except by marrying her. Not that I'm really any different than your other women. You could have used your charm; I'm sure it would have worked. But it was a question of conscience, wasn't it? I was too near home." She knew she was saying too much. His eyes were impaling her and his face had gone savagely white. But it was like running at great speed down a steep hill, once started she couldn't stop. "You want me. I can feel the vibrations of your lust reaching out to me right now. You're hungry for me. *That's* why you married me. But you'll never have me. Never, never, never. Go to her. I don't care."

"Am I supposed to read any sense in this outburst?" he said, his narrowed eyes hard and unyielding on hers. His fingers wound around her wrists so tightly she thought he must stop her pulse beat. His voice cracked against her cheek with the fury of a whip. "Go to her, you say? Who are you talking about? Explain yourself."

"The woman who was on your bed when I came in," she informed him scornfully, refusing to be intimidated by his strength.

"What woman?"

"What woman do you think? A woman with black hair wearing black satin pajamas. I didn't stop to ask her name."

His breath sucked in harshly. "That sounds as if it could be Justine Hyland."

"Sounds as if it could be?" she screamed at him. "Do you mean there's more than one black-haired woman who could be waiting for you on your bed?"

"No, it's got to be Justine. But she wasn't there at my invitation and she's never been waiting for me before."

"Oh yes? Do you expect me to believe that?"

"It's the truth. You little fool, don't you see that you've been set up? Justine did it so that you would lose your temper and behave in exactly the hot-headed way you are doing."

"She wouldn't have had time. She didn't know I was coming," she protested, quavering, doubtful.

"It's typical of Justine's scheming brain." Did she detect a glitter of laughter in his eyes, as if he applauded the woman's audacity? "How much notice do you think she'd need? Word obviously got to her the moment we arrived, which would give her ample time to get up here and give you the reception she did. Think about it. You've got all night."

Without another word he dropped her wrists, turned, and walked toward the door.

"Where are you going?" she asked with a stirring of panic and possibly regret.

"You've all night to think about that too."

The door slammed shut after him.

Chapter Three

She flung herself down on the bed. Even in her anguish she was squeamish enough to choose the other bed, the one without the scent of the other woman's perfume lingering on the spread. The thought of lying where that woman had lain filled her with revulsion.

She closed her eyes, but all she could see was the set of David's dark, concerned face—the swift searching look in his eyes as he tried to find a cause for her behavior, and then that look changing to cold anger and icy contempt.

She would not listen to him . . . would not listen to reason, even. All she'd been able to think of was that sensuous snake of a woman in her seductive black satin pajamas. Had she—what was her name? Justine?—set Petrina up? It was possible. The word that David had brought a wife with him would have swept through the hotel like wildfire. Did Justine work in the hotel? It seemed more credible that she was involved in the hotel in some way than that David was indulging in an affair with a guest. Had a colleague raced to tell her that David had returned, bringing a bride with him? And had she decided to do the woman scorned routine and dash along to his room to give the bride an unpleasant reception? She would have nothing to lose. If the story had turned out to be untrue, if her informant had been mistaken or was playing a joke on her, Justine would have been there to give David a warm welcome.

Perhaps she was giving him that warm welcome at this very moment, stroking her hands over the muscled virility of his lean body, tempting him to laugh with her at the childish hot-headedness of the silly little girl he'd married.

Married. The word hung in her mind. She and David were married, and she had no idea what he expected in a wife.

Oh, dear heaven, what had she done? Why hadn't she let David tell her who Justine was, and then she wouldn't be battling against supposition?

She swung her legs off the bed and crossed the narrow strip to the other bed. With shaking hands she smoothed the bedspread back to its immaculate un-touched image, as if by pressing out the wrinkles she could evict from her mind that black-haired woman with her slinky hips and her sneering red splash of a mouth.

Before she went back to her own bed, she wandered out into the sitting room in the forlorn hope that perhaps David had made a bed for himself there. He wasn't there—neither was he on the balcony.

She'd been a fool to boil up like that, sending David away, depriving herself of his arms on her wedding night, causing pain and humiliation to them both. If only he had stayed. She might not have had his love, but he, had he only known it, would have had all of hers.

He had to sleep somewhere. Someone would know they'd slept apart on their wedding night. As she saw it, he had two courses open to him. He would either go straight to Justine, or he would get another room allocated for himself. Someone—Justine, the receptionist, a chambermaid—would talk. It was too good a morsel not to be divulged.

Light was trailing across the sky before the release of sleep came, and even then her dreams must have been troubled because twice her eyes flicked open with a start to realize that the noise that had awakened her was her own whimpering. Eventually she must have dropped off into a sleep that was so deep that it seemed nothing could rouse her. But something did. This time it was not her own sobs that woke her, but a hand biting cruelly into her shoulder.

She recoiled sharply, and then David's voice sliced into her awareness. "I'm not going to strike you, if that's what you're afraid of. I've brought your morning coffee." He set it down on the bedside table and subjected her to a long critical appraisal. "You look ghastly. Your mascara's run and you've got two black eyes."

Despite her brightly colored hair, which looked more golden than copper in the polishing rays of the morning sun, her eyelashes were naturally dark and silky. Sometimes she used a smudge of coloring on her eyelids, but she had never used mascara in her life. The two black eyes David spoke of were the bruising shadows her night of stress and remorse had given to her.

Had there been the tiniest glimmer of kindness or

forgiveness in his face, she would have let it all come spilling out, everything about the terrible night she'd spent and how she realized how silly she'd been and that she loved him and would he please give her another chance. But no way could she make this plea while he looked at her with such icy contempt.

What a gullible fool she had been. She had played right into Justine's hands. She remembered with horror the words of abuse she'd flung at him last night. She'd taunted him, said that he'd only married her to possess her and vowed that he never would. Couldn't he look at her now and see that her eyes were rescinding that statement? She had spoken impetuously in her wild rage, spoken against every inclination of her heart and of her body, which had ached for him then even as she sent him away, which ached for him now, even as he looked at her with eyes full of cold distaste.

She was going to fight Justine, although she didn't know how. She knew that she was at a severe disadvantage. Although it was a new game to her, Justine would be an accomplished hand at this sort of thing. There was little she could do at the moment because she wasn't calm enough. If she tried to tell him all that was in her heart, she would never be able to contain her tears. David despised tears. Tears were a child's way of manipulating a situation; they demonstrated an inability to cope. This wasn't a game for juveniles. It would hardly serve her purpose to prove that she was a child. It was a woman's game, and she must compete as a woman. That barred her from telling David that the black under her eyes was shadow and not yesterday's mascara.

She yawned. "I forgot to remove my makeup."

"You also forgot to take off your dress," he said, his eyes full of scorn.

That hadn't been very clever of her. Her eyes wandered away from his, swept across the untouched supper cart and fell unhappily on the unwrinkled smoothness of the other bed. "David, I know why you're attacking me, and I don't blame you."

The blue eyes were enigmatic as they surveyed her beneath a sarcastically lifted brow. "That's magnanimous of you."

"Please don't talk down to me. I won't grovel, David. I'm trying to be fair. Make things right for you. I know I can't undo what happened last night—"

He cut in snidely to say, "Don't you mean what didn't happen?"

She continued steadfastly, endeavoring to ignore the interruption as she paid the full price of his condemnation with inner remorse and shame. "I would like to do all in my power to make amends now."

"My little Pet." The insult of the endearment, because it was not said in a caressing voice, was carried a step further as his stripping glance sensuously stroked her body. "Are you inviting me into your bed? Making yourself available to me now?"

She held on to her anger, although not without great difficulty. She could feel it steaming up inside. She knew that he was humiliating her because she had humiliated him last night. By accepting it she was, in a small way, making atonement.

"If that's what you want, yes. I was thinking more of appearances though. If we ruffled the other bed up, it would look as though you'd slept there. And we could toss some food about on the plates, to make it appear as though we'd eaten some of it."

"And pour the champagne down the bath outlet? You're bothering about nothing. The maid will think we were too hungry for other things to waste time on food, too intoxicated with one another to require drink. As for my bed not being slept in, doesn't that suggest a full night of mad, passionate debauchery in your bed?"

She bit hard on her lip. She must not retaliate. She must remain seemingly sweet and docile while he played his cat-and-mouse game, and then she would not blame herself, as she had blamed herself for last night. If he demanded recompense, he could have it.

Her good intentions crumbled as he made a move toward her. She flinched away instinctively.

"I was only going to hand you your coffee, which you haven't touched yet. Still, it will be cold by now, so I won't. What did you think I was going to do, *Pet*-rina? This?" His hand moved around to locate the tag on her zip. She felt a stroking movement down her spine and her dress lost its cling.

He assisted her arms out and the material fell away and curled around her hips. He lifted her out of it; she felt like a doll. It was wrong, all wrong. The look on his face as he continued to undress her in this cold, calculating way made it distasteful. His mouth ought not to have been held steady in this grim expression, but should have tantalized and excited her as it brushed gently and searchingly over her face and neck, whispering her name between kisses. The tender warmth of his expression should have tempted her into a crazy vortex of feeling and heightened awareness, instead of which the cold savagery of his movements washed over her in icy waves, provoking panic in her throat and turning her body into a resisting block of frigidity.

Her thoughts were locked in argument with her emotions. Her mind instilled its wish to remain passive, but her body could not make the pretense and stiffened

48

in rejection. It would not be used like this and it repelled him.

"I knew it! This is exactly how I expected you to act. Although I must admit," he said in a cool and sneering drawl, "I thought you were going to call my bluff. I was wondering how far I would have to go before *I* had to repel *you*."

Then, and only then, did it occur to her that his mocking eyes had never left her face; his impersonal hands had removed her clothes without touching her body.

"You are despicable," she said, drawing a harsh breath.

"I would have had to agree with you if I'd taken you up on your offer. Not that there was much risk of that. I've never been so hard up that I've had to take an unwilling woman to bed, and I'm not likely to change my habits now. I merely wanted to prove that to you."

"All right, point taken."

"Is it? Has it got through to you that the big jealous act you put on last night was unnecessary?"

It wasn't an act, her brain screamed. "I *was* jeal—"

He interrupted. "All you had to say to me was that you'd married me to get out of a tight corner but that you couldn't go through with the full marriage commitment, and I would have understood. After all, I did offer you this . . . bargain."

So that's what he thought. He thought she'd cheated him, lied to him. "I didn't—"

"I'm not the sex-starved fiend you seem to have labeled me. Did you want to say something? Tell me over breakfast. Right now I suggest you take a shower. A cold one. You look as if you need cooling off. Join me in the dining room as soon as you're ready."

"I'm not hungry. If you don't mind, I'll skip breakfast," she said, speaking quickly in her desperation to complete a full sentence, and felt silly when her words fell into the lengthy pause he allowed.

At full effective length he said, "Oh, but I do mind. You are my wife and I want you by my side."

She sighed in heavy exasperation, knowing she might as well give in with reasonable grace and come first as last. "Please don't leave me to find my own way down to the dining room. Please wait for me."

A grim smile came to his lips. "Yes, all right. Don't be long."

"I won't," she promised.

Was that it? Had she somehow found the key? She had told him she wasn't going to grovel, but something about the set of his face had replied, "We'll see about that." Was he going to make her grovel every step of the way?

She pulled her robe on, and with its soft folds about her her dignity returned. As she walked toward the bathroom she felt a certain satisfaction in knowing that his eyes could not resist following her. The feel of them boring into her back gave her spirits a lift. He had chosen to punish her by remaining impervious. But perhaps he'd punished himself as well, because he wasn't as impervious as he tried to make out.

Unpacking was another of last night's omissions. After a cool, invigorating shower, she dragged a cream dress from her suitcase, giving thanks for the un-crushable quality of the material. It was built on the skimpy lines of a sun dress, with shoelace shoulder straps. She confined her makeup to a dab of moisturizing lotion, brushed the tangles out of her hair, and joined David on the balcony, where he had chosen to wait for her.

Last night, in the total darkness, she had looked out at nothing, thrilling to the sound of the sea, supposing it was wearing itself out on the rocks beneath the balcony.

Actually, the sea was further away than she had thought, separated from the building not only by a narrow strip of sand but also by the hotel swimming pool, which was edged with brightly colored loungers under the shade of garish umbrellas or trees that looked artificial, as if they'd been uprooted from their natural setting, as indeed they had, and planted there for effect.

"You don't like it?" David said, observing her face.

"It's not to my taste," she admitted.

"The general public disagrees with you," he informed her gravely.

She shrugged her shoulders in disdain.

"What's that meant to imply?"

"Merely what I said before—that you are loyal to your employer."

"My employer?" he said, frowning.

Replying to his tone of query and ignoring that prohibitive frown, she said, "The man you work for. The opportunist who took advantage of my father's misfortune to make his own fortune."

"You're not being fair. There's no middle course, Petrina. It's either up or down. If he hadn't learned something from your father's mistakes, then he would have gone down too."

"How can you defend him? He's nothing but an unscrupulous profiteer without taste or finer feelings."

"I admit it does look as though he took advantage of the situation to make an exorbitant profit, but there's more to it than that. Someone had to step in with a salvaging plan. There would have been little to choose from, whoever had come in."

She stubbornly refused to believe that. "If only he hadn't tried to reach too high," she said bitterly. "Ambition is a virus. It kills."

"It wasn't ambition that killed your father—failure did," he pointed out somberly.

She awarded him a brief glance. She didn't want him to see the look on her face, to let him know by the flicker of intelligence that crossed her features that he was right. Ambition had been the breath of life to her father, his inspiration and mainstay—failure had been the executioner.

"I don't suppose this one hotel will make much difference," she said haughtily.

He grabbed her by the shoulders and swung her around so he could look deep into her eyes, as though willing her to understand something she was unconsciously rejecting.

"You're hurting me," she said, but her plea went unnoticed and his hands retained their hold.

"It's not one hotel. It had to be an extravagant plan of salvation or it wouldn't have worked. The Hotel León is the premier hotel in a hotel complex served by shops and bars and all the other vulgar amenities that pull in the tourists. The greedy opportunist, the profiteer you despise so much, has pandered to the ostentatious whims and predilections of the paying public. Forget your father's dream. That died three years ago. Three years, do you hear? It's taken three years of blood and sweat to achieve what's taken its place. Three years to build Chimera up to what it is now, and this is only the beginning." One hand released itself from her shoulder and clamped on to her chin. He twisted her face around to make her look down at the colorful gaudiness of the swimming pool scene. "This is the reality of Chimera. Accept it."

"I can't. You're asking too much."

"I'm not, considering."

"What?"

"Nothing." His mouth snapped shut, as if he'd gone too deep into the subject, saying more than he'd intended. "I'm hungry."

She found herself being roughly propelled in front of him and marched out of the suite.

Before they got to the elevator he had regained his composure, and with it his mocking tongue. "You could put on a smile. I wouldn't like it to be thought that I was losing my touch."

She cast a warning glance in the direction of the elevator attendant. It wasn't Ignacio this morning, but a boy of similar height and age.

"It's all right—he doesn't understand a word of English. He'd be very dim not to understand your face though. The frostiness of a frown is the same in any language."

"Is that better?" she said, lifting her mouth in a hard, brittle little grimace.

"If it's the best you can do. If we weren't in a public place I'd have a stab at improving it," he said, mocking her scruples.

She wasn't meant to reply; she wasn't given time. His hand smoothed down her back and curved in to fit around her waist. Her chin lifted in an automatic gesture of surprise, to find his eyes were waiting to ambush hers. Cold, cruel, tormenting. She wrenched free of his hold. The elevator doors opened and she stepped out, not caring if they did look like a couple in the throes of a raging argument. Why should she care about appearances when he so obviously didn't?

He guided her across the dining room to a table with a reserved sign on it. It was already occupied by two people whose heads were close together in conversation—a girl in her mid-twenties and a man a year or two older. It would appear that these two were going to be their table companions and she was glad to leave the tangled torment of her thoughts for the moment.

Even sitting, it was apparent that the girl was above average height and as thin as a whip. She was a brown-eyed blond with a clever, fine-boned face that looked good at the angle it was presented to Petrina, and even better when her chin swiveled around and her mouth warmed in a smile of greeting.

David had started the introductions and so she delayed looking at the man.

"Pet," he said, "this is my secretary, the cool and efficient Miss Virginia Lewis, who keeps me on my toes."

"Good to know you, Mrs. Palmer. And it's actually the other way around; your husband keeps me on my toes."

The man intervened. "For once she's right. You can see by the length of her that she's stretched to the limit."

"The joker is Robert Dawson, my chief assistant," David put in.

"Happy to meet you, Mrs. Palmer." He had already stood up and now he extended his hand. He had a big warm handshake that matched his round, genial face and his huge physique.

"How do you do, Mr. Dawson?" Petrina acknowledged as her smile found itself without difficulty.

"Please call me Bob," he said.

"And I'm Ginny," the tall woman threw in.

All through the meal, Bob and Ginny sniped back and forth at each other, and Petrina wondered how on earth they ever managed to work together. At first she was totally bewildered by their behavior; she'd never met their likes before. But then a curious notion filtered into her mind. They were doing it on purpose to alleviate the tension they expected to exist between her and David. They knew about the disharmony.

Could they have been quick enough to tune in to the mood from the other side of the dining room? No, they'd been too absorbed in their own conversation to observe anything, and had even seemed surprised when they realized they were about to have company. And they'd gone into their double act straight away, before they'd had time to sniff out the strained atmosphere. It pointed to prior knowledge.

How much they knew was the teaser. Did they know that David hadn't spent the night with her? There was a shrewd suspicion in her mind that the answer to that was yes. Did they both know? Or was one of them taking the cue from the other? Could the news have traveled so fast or . . . ?

The natural conclusion to that thought raised an intriguing possibility. Perhaps David hadn't gone tearing into Justine's arms. Perhaps he hadn't alerted someone to find another room for him. Perhaps he'd doubled up with an old friend. But which old friend? Whose door had he knocked on—Bob's or Ginny's?

Her emotions were playing tug-of-war over this new concept. A short while ago she would have staked her life on the fact that if someone had provided her with a new theory to supplant the one that David had spent the night with Justine she would never have believed it. But that was before she met Ginny.

Ginny wasn't beautiful, but she was certainly attractive—even with her hair tied back with that piece of brown ribbon, though Petrina thought a softer frame would have suited her face better. She was very tall and very thin, but not unattractive at all. How could someone with such a sexless shape manage to look like such a very sexy lady?

The penetration of her glance drew Ginny's eyes, and the other woman grinned across at her. Oh, help, Petrina thought, she's nice. I like her.

After breakfast, David, Ginny, and Bob disappeared into the downstairs office that was tucked behind the reception desk. Left to her own devices, Petrina decided to take her thoughts for a walk.

The hotel guests were already claiming loungers by the pool for a day-long vigil of sun worship. As she threaded her way through the hotel grounds she felt conspicuously pale among so many mahogany-colored bodies.

When she reached the beach she took off her sandals, wishing she'd thought to put her swimsuit on beneath her sun dress. Following her natural inclination and the curve of the coastline, she left the hotel complex and the shops behind.

The sea was a dazzle of diamonds. The heat of the sun on the back of her head was overpowering. She would have to change her English money into the local currency and set about buying some necessities. Besides the already longed-for sun hat, she needed sunglasses and some screening cream for her very fair skin.

She walked beyond the lion's head and was halfway down the goat's body when she decided that, much as the serpent's tail beckoned her—the coastline swished sharply away in its serpent's tail shape and she couldn't see what was beyond—until she was better equipped and more acclimatized to the hot sun, it was foolish to go any further.

The sea looked very tempting. She didn't know about currents and things, but there were no red flags up, so presumably it was safe to bathe. The strapless bra she was wearing under her sun dress was the same color as her panties; no one would know she wasn't wearing a bikini. In any case, no one was close enough to see. The crowds apparently chose to stay within a tight radius of the hotel complex and she had this part of the beach to herself.

She flung off her sun dress, dropped it delicately onto the white sand, and plunged into the sea. It was heavenly. She floated and flipped and curved and played, a cross between a mermaid, with her hair streaming out around her face, and a porpoise, with her sense of fun.

She half expected to run into trouble of some sort. It would be just her luck for a stray dog to pop up from nowhere and run off with her dress. Her undies were more modest than the average bikini, but she didn't fancy returning to the hotel clad just in them. But no, in this the fates were on her side, and nothing unforeseen happened.

She waded out of the sea, feeling gloriously tingly and alive, dried off in the sun, put on her sun dress, and made her way back to the hotel. She felt slightly light-headed. She hoped she hadn't stayed out too long in the sun on her first day.

There was no sign of David when she got back so presumably he was still working. She washed the salt water out of her hair and unpacked her suitcase while it dried. She put on a fresh dress and went down to the dining room in search of lunch. She realized that she had hardly thought of her problems all morning—and that it had been wonderful.

Only Bob occupied the reserved corner table. He waved her over.

"David and Ginny still have their noses to the grindstone. There's a heck of a lot of work to be done. What do you think of Chimera? Does it live up to expectations?"

He was grinning like a self-satisfied little boy; it was so obvious he expected her to go into raptures over what they had achieved. She didn't know what to say. It wasn't that she didn't have the courage to stand up for her own beliefs, it was a case of not wanting to dampen his enthusiasm.

"It's . . . very . . ." She gulped and started again. "Actually, I'm lost for words."

He nodded in delight. "I know just what you mean, Mrs. Palmer," he said, knowing no such thing. "You wouldn't believe the plans that are in the works to keep the guests happily entertained and the bookings rolling in all year round."

"It sounds interesting," she said.

She knew that David was standing behind her chair even before he spoke. She felt him the moment he entered the dining room; now she felt his breath on her cheek as he drawled silkily, "Interesting, did you say? That doesn't sound like you at all, Pet." Over the top of her stiffly held head he informed Bob, "My wife thinks it's very lazy of people to rely on someone else to provide their entertainment. She is a very primitive lady. She prefers the natural pleasures, don't you, Pet?" The rubbing motion of the hand on the back of her neck was as sensuous as the voice in her ear.

The color ran up her skin. He must know he was embarrassing both her and Bob.

Bob said, affably enough despite his obvious discomfort, "There are lots of unspoiled places on the island, Mrs. Palmer. And I know you'll just love—"

David's amused voice cut in, "'Mrs. Palmer' sounds much too formal. I'm sure my wife won't mind your using her given name or its diminutive."

"I'd prefer it," she said gratefully.

"Thanks, so would I," Bob admitted. "So, as I was saying, Pet—"

Once again David cut him off. This time the rebuke was not gentle—it was sharp, with a skimming of unkind amusement. "Not Pet. You can take your choice between Petrina or Trina. She's nobody's Pet but mine."

Petrina's fingers curled furiously into the palms of her hands. His meaning couldn't have been clearer or more insulting if he'd come right out and said "nobody's plaything but mine." It would have been more honest to say that because that's what he had meant to imply.

"I'm sorry," Bob said, a gentle frown on his face. "I meant no offense; I thought Pet was a general nickname. Which alternative are you happiest with?" he asked directly of Petrina.

"Trina," she replied quite definitely.

That lunch was not an easy meal. Petrina was smoldering. She wondered how long David was going to punish her for last night, and how long she could stand it before she rounded back on him. Ginny came to join them, but even her talkative presence couldn't totally iron out the taut silences. Ginny didn't make any gauche inquiries, and beyond throwing Bob a confused look, which he answered with a slight shrug of his huge shoulders, she rattled on gamely as if nothing was amiss. The only reassuring thing, thought Petrina, was that David seemed no more interested in Ginny than he was in Bob. Perhaps, she hoped, she had been mistaken in that after all.

Later in the day, Petrina was just leaving the reception counter, having changed her English money into the local currency, when Bob ambled up. It was just a thought, but it seemed to her that he'd been waiting for the opportunity to have a word, although he made it seem as if he'd stumbled upon her by chance.

"You want to watch the sun. I'm sure your nose has caught it."

She didn't say that she feared it was more than her nose that had caught it. Instead she nodded sagely. "I'm on my way to the shops now. I'm going to buy myself the largest sun hat I can find."

"Sensible girl. The hotel shopping facilities are quite good, although you'll probably get a larger selection if you wander farther afield to the shopping precinct." He bit on his lip. "Trina?"

"Yes, Bob?" she said, meeting his eyes.

"I'm probably out of line saying this, but that husband of yours isn't the bear he made himself out to be at lunchtime."

"No?"

"No. All this—"he gestured at the hotel around them—"hasn't just come about. It's been hard work, and he's the only one of us who hasn't taken a holiday for the full three-year stint. Apart from sneaking a couple of days off to fetch you, that is. And then he had to make the time up, although I'm not sure whether that wasn't dedication to idiocy rather than to duty. I'm not just speaking like this about him behind his back; I told him to his face last night. I said I couldn't see the sense of us working ourselves bleary-eyed into the small hours, no matter how snowed under we were. I don't think either of us quite realized what the time was or we'd have quit. And then it was so late that he didn't want to disturb you, so he sacked out on the spare bed in my room."

"Thank you, Bob. Thank you for putting me in the picture."

"Don't mention it."

She had no intention of mentioning it. The last thing she intended to do was let David know that she knew where he'd spent last night.

Chapter Four

It was always good to have a friend. No matter how many friends a person has, there's always room for one more, Petrina thought. In her position, uprooted from all the links of childhood, vulnerable in her new surroundings, it was especially comforting to have found a friend in Bob.

She hadn't known, until Bob let it out, that the three of them—David, Ginny, and Bob—had been locked together in this project for the full three years since it was taken over from her father. That was a lot of testing-out-theories, sharing-ideas, and getting-to-know-each-other time.

Even though she could go them one better than that—she had known David all her life—somehow it wasn't the same. She had been the little girl he tolerated because of a long-standing family friendship.

When things had gone wrong, David's father had been her staunch and loving ally, and somehow David had inherited from his father the feeling of responsibility toward her.

She didn't want to be a burden or a responsibility to anyone. Had she been wrong in accepting David's proposal? Despite what he thought, she hadn't married him to get out of a tight corner. She would have made out. She was too much her father's daughter to be out of the running forever. She had married him for that most corny and wonderful of reasons: she loved him. She always would. If only she knew for sure why he had married her. Had it been only to satisfy the attraction he felt, or was there something more . . . ?

All the time she'd been thinking, she'd been walking. The temporary cessation of her thoughts was marked by an unhappy sigh and the knowledge that she had arrived at the hotel shopping area. It was not just one shop, but a mini-precinct of its own that catered to just about every need. There was a shop that sold film and sunglasses and lipsticks and lotions and a shop that sold trinkets and souvenirs, from baubles for the ears to child-high donkeys. There was a hairdressing shop and a newsstand, and at the very end of the arcade was a ladies' fashion boutique displaying a pile of sun hats.

She went in. After trying on several, she settled for a pale parchment-colored wide-brimmed hat in squashy straw that could be pushed into a beach bag and still come up smiling. Her eyes had been straying toward a charming and artistically arranged collection of lingerie, but they quickly came back to base when she realized that Justine Hyland had entered the shop. Petrina had been toying with the thought of buying a more attractive nightgown to replace the two functional cotton ones she'd brought with her, but she was certainly not going to choose anything so intimate while that woman was watching.

She managed to make it known to the assistant, a pretty little Spanish girl with laughing, liquid eyes and the sweetest manner, that she was going to wear the sun hat and didn't want it wrapped, but when she opened her purse and tried to pay for it the girl became quite excited in her refusal. Petrina was at a complete loss to know what she was doing wrong. Was she offering insufficient money? She wasn't used to the currency yet. If she'd erred on the generous side, surely the girl could give her the correct change. Unless she was out of change. Was that it?

"I think you need help," Justine Hyland finally came forward to say.

Petrina nodded helplessly, although she wished the offer to act as interpreter had come from someone else. "I don't know what I'm doing wrong."

"The assistant has recognized you as David's wife. She doesn't dare take your money because David has instructed her that anything you want must be charged to his account."

"Oh, I see. Thank you. I didn't know."

"Didn't you?" Justine's elegant black eyebrows rose in eloquent meaning. "Something else David has been remiss in telling you."

Petrina chin lifted. "As he was remiss about telling me of your existence? Is that what you mean?"

Justine's smile was sweetly gloating, but she said nothing.

Petrina's eyes glanced across to where the little Spanish assistant stood. "Am I right in thinking she doesn't understand a word of English."

"Not a word," Justine confirmed.

"In that case, Miss Hyland, I think you are filthy-minded and despicable."

Justine's scarlet mouth thinned in menace. "That was your biggest mistake to date. You'll rue saying that, Mrs. Palmer. It isn't even as though your statement is correct."

"You mean you're not despicable?" Petrina challenged in as steady a tone as her fury would allow.

"Oh, I'm despicable. That's not the inaccuracy. I'm not a miss. There's a Mr. Hyland, and Geoffrey is a very vindictive man. I shouldn't complain, because I certainly have my faults. My worst failing is my indiscretion. David has been asking me for a long time to apply more caution in the matter of our friendship. He said if I didn't mend my ways, in view of my husband's power and wealth, he would have to take positive action to protect himself. Would you say the sudden acquisition of a wife comes under that heading?"

The belief that Justine wasn't a guest but was involved in the hotel in some way still held firm in Petrina's mind, but not as an employee. Her husband was a man of power and wealth. David had felt the need to protect himself. Did this add up to anything? Could Justine's husband, this Geoffrey Hyland, be the opportunist who bought her father out? Was he David's boss? And, worse, had David only married her to shield his affair with Justine and protect them from Geoffrey Hyland's wrath?

"Incidentally," Justine purred, "I couldn't help but notice your interest in the lingerie stand. If you want any help with choosing what David finds exciting, I'll be happy to oblige."

Not averse to showing her own claws, now that the battle lines were drawn, and feeling that this was the moment to begin to fight back, Petrina said, "I'm sure you're always happy to oblige."

Almost as if Petrina had made no comment, Justine said with silky smoothness, at the same time fingering a confection of a nightgown in a delicate moonbeam shade of oyster-pink that coincided with Petrina's own taste, "For example, he would find you irresistible in this."

"Too bad," Petrina said, goaded beyond either reason or inclination, "because this is the one I'm buying." She pointed haphazardly, and almost died when she saw which nightgown she'd picked out. It was a whisper of erotic black lace. It took a lot of defiance and courage to stick to her unhappy choice and motion the assistant to wrap it for her.

With her sun hat pressed firmly down on her head, and the incredible purchase in her hand, she swept past Justine and out of the shop.

She had never for a moment thought the bedroom act was a complete bluff on Justine's part, but she'd consoled herself with the thought that David had married *her* and not Justine. Now, it seemed, she knew the reason for that.

David had married her to protect his job *and* his affair. What husband was going to be jealously watchful of a newly married man? David had really excelled himself in deviousness this time. And it all fit together too well not to be true.

She had intended to buy sunglasses and some very necessary sun creams and lotions to pamper her skin after its exposure to the sun, but she didn't feel composed enough to choose with care, and so she swung around again, back to the hotel, and went straight up to the suite.

In the privacy of the bedroom she tore the dainty wrapping off her parcel, held the vampish whisper of lace in her hands for an agonized second, and tossed it in disgust down on her bed. The only reason she didn't toss herself after it was because a weeping session would serve no useful purpose.

A maid had apparently come by to collect the dirty laundry. David, of course, knew the routine and had left his things in a neat pile. Also scooped up had been several discarded items of Petrina's. Had her permission been asked she would have said no, preferring to do her own small things. As she looked helplessly around her, she resolved that next time she would beat the chambermaid to it.

She felt so useless. She didn't like to think that other people were working while she had nothing to do. Looking over the balcony rail down to the swimming pool below, she saw that the gaily colored loungers were still occupied by the sun worshippers. Such inactivity wasn't in her line at all. She looked at her watch. Although it was still on the early side to think about getting dressed for dinner, the day was too far advanced to consider doing something that would take any length of time. David would be coming up soon, though heaven alone knew in what kind of mood. It would be an open act of defiance not to be there when he came.

That thought was all she needed to jam her sun hat on her head and give the brim a jaunty twist before making her way down and leaving the hotel again.

This time she circled around the back of the hotel and walked past several other hotels, which, although not quite as large, were almost identical to the Hotel León with their sea-facing balconies, huge swimming pools, attractively laid out sun terraces, children's playgrounds, and sports areas. As the brochures said, something for everybody—everybody but Petrina.

She located a road that wound interestingly up into the mountains. It crossed her mind that if she reached higher ground she might be able to see the piece of land that flicked around in the shape of a serpent's tail. But distances are deceptive, as she was to find out. Although she climbed to a fair height and had a panoramic view of the hotel complex in the lion's head and the stretch of sand that was, in her mind, at least, the goat's body, the peculiar twist of the coastline still concealed the serpent's tail from her.

It was tantalizing to have come so far without reward. It was becoming an obsession with her to probe this secret place. She sat on a rock, getting her breath back and fanning her burning cheeks with her sun hat. She felt sick and dizzy. She would have blamed this on the steep climb but for the fact that this feeling had been coming and going since lunchtime.

Although the secret of the serpent's tail was not revealed to her, her toil did not go unrewarded. The sun slid into the sea. It was so dramatically sudden that she felt she should have heard the plop.

She had seen sunsets before, but never one of this splendor. It was an unexpected manifestation of shot-silk colors spinning across the sky in bolts of gaudy orange, imperial purple, and rich dragon's blood red. The beauty of it held her in silent homage. Even when it was over, and the twilight stillness fell, she sat a while longer before reluctantly beginning the downhill journey.

Stones and ruts, easily spotted in the daytime, assaulted the soles of her feet and jarred her spine. The need to tread warily slowed her pace and she knew she was going to be disgracefully late getting back.

She opened the door of their suite to find that David had already showered and changed and was fuming in that predominantly male fashion. A woman waiting on a man's inclination to put in an appearance is a much more patient and tranquil creature, Petrina told herself.

She pelted in, hoping to slip past him, but his hand came out to bar her progress just a few steps short of the sanctuary of the bathroom.

"Where have you been?" he demanded.

"Walking," she snapped back in defiance.

"In the dark?" His voice was ominously icy and had a chilling effect on her nerves.

With less fervor, she said, "That sort of fell on me." She was immediately sorry that she had allowed herself to be intimidated and stoked up the heat again to say, "Obviously it wasn't dark when I set off." Her mouth curved in the pretense of a smile that was more like a sneer as she added in empty apology, "I'm sorry."

"The devil you are."

"The dining room is open until eleven. I don't see what all the fuss is about."

"Don't you?" His breath sucked in harshly. "Didn't it occur to you that I might be worried?"

She gave him a long, keen look that traced the hard set of his dark face, trying to determine something that gave credence to his concern in the unwavering straightness of his mouth, striving to penetrate the harshness in his eyes. She could find nothing to cheer her; she could not see one flicker of solicitude anywhere on his face. His caring wasn't for her, but for his own creature comforts.

She spat at him in contemptuous and rash disregard, "If you were in such a hurry for your meal, I'm surprised you didn't follow your usual custom of leaving me to find my own way down. That certainly worked well enough at lunch."

"You don't have to rub it in. I'm aware that I've neglected you. Things—tentative ideas and explorations into new ventures that have been gently simmering for months—have suddenly come to the boil. I haven't chosen to leave you to your own devices, it's not up to me, and it goes especially against the grain to ignore you this way while you're feeling raw. I know you're grieving over the loss of your father. I wish I could see some evidence of the pace slackening, but I can't."

His hand stroked upward through his hair in a weary gesture that was at odds with his usual positive assurance. It was such a human thing to do that she almost followed it up by allowing her hand to imitate his actions and lose her fingers in the bouncing virility of his dark hair. She didn't dare, because his reference to the recent loss of her father made her feel too emotional. She couldn't make a tender move toward David without dissolving into tears, and that weakness was definitely not permitted. She'd already made up her mind that there must be no childish tears in this woman's game.

So she said, somehow managing to appear to be calm and in complete control of herself, "I don't mind so much now that you've explained. Why don't you go a step further? Instead of shutting me out, why don't you tell me about these new ideas and ventures?"

Perhaps her cover was too good and her seeming calm infuriated him and he was goaded into making the attack. Perhaps it had nothing to do with her manner at all, but that he was furious with himself for letting her penetrate his steely indifference. Or perhaps, the painful thought intruded, it was because he wanted as little to do with her as possible and resented every minute that her presence kept him away from Justine Hyland.

"Don't you think the situation between us is explosive enough as it is? There are things you aren't fit to know. If I told you just the half of what the future holds for your precious Chimera, you'd hate me forever, if you don't already. You call it commercialism, as if it's a dirty word, and you treat me as though I'm committing murder on mankind. Yet the changes are inevitable. Nothing stands still, neither people nor places. In this unspoiled world of yours no one should be permitted to grow older than six or seven, and then the beautiful illusion could be preserved. We could all maintain implicit belief in fairy tales and live in a land where you break off a piece of the gingerbread house when you're hungry, and the prince lives happily ever after on a kiss from his fair princess."

At some time during the tirade he had grabbed her by the shoulders. His blue eyes burned into hers in a bitter attack on her nerves. Instead of flinching away, she held steady under the violence of his stare. She was not being brave; she was held mesmerised in his grip. Even in anger, his eyes lusted for her and his spell was frightening, forcing her, as it did, to respond.

Her head tilted back; her hands moved up to wind around his neck, and her fingers linked to make a ring. She heard his agonized groan. His hands followed the course hers had taken, finding her tightly clasped fingers. His hands briefly covered hers, then separated, and a finger trailed down the length of each uplifted arm, scalding her senses, trailing fire down her skin with their light touch.

"You put your arms up around my neck like this once before," he said. His voice was throaty with emotion. "Do you remember?"

"I remember," she said.

She remembered all too vividly. She had been only eighteen and she had not yet had a chance to learn the wiles of womanhood, and in her youth and ignorance she had declared her love for him. It had broken her heart when he rejected her because she was a child. It was three years ago, but it might have been yesterday. She had tried to forget, but twice within a week the memory had been forced back upon her, and still it hurt. The tangy fresh smell of his after-shave, that distinctive blend of sage, laurel, and oak moss, was still in her nose.

She said shakily, "I think you're wearing the same after-shave."

He slanted her an odd look. His voice was grave and rueful. "I probably am. I'm faithful that way. When I find something I like, I stick to it. Do you remember what I called it when you made a ring of your arms round my neck?"

"You called it the ring of seduction," she said huskily.

"I resisted it then because you were too young. You're not a child any longer; furthermore, you're my wife. I'm not about to resist it now."

His fingers had stilled on her shoulderblades; now they separated again to continue their journey. One hand traveled down her back to hold her close; the other curved around to anchor her chin. "Be warned— you're not going to make rings around me now and get away with it."

"I don't want to get away with anything," she said

hoarsely. "Were you really worried about me because I was late in returning to the hotel?"

"Of course I was worried, you little fool."

"What could have happened to me?" she scoffed, delighting in his caring, the preliminary love play of words, and the disturbing nearness of his body.

His eyes were dark with meaning. "Do you want it in lurid detail? There are places on this island where it isn't safe for a woman to be alone after dark."

"You're saying that I could have slipped on the rough ground and hurt my ankle? Or I could have fallen down a ravine and not been able to get up again and I would have had to wait until you came to find me?" she teased pertly.

"I should have found you, wherever you were. But don't treat it as a joke because such a thing is possible. You could have been lying in a gully somewhere, seriously injured and in great pain, and it might have been hours—or days—before I discovered you. But you know perfectly well that's not what I meant."

"I don't know anything of the sort." She looked at him from under her lashes. "Do you mean someone, a man, might have come across me while I was wandering in the dark, helpless and alone, and taken advantage of me? Tell me, I'm curious to know."

"I know you're curious. And if I'd been that man and found you wandering in some dark and lonely place, you'd be curious no more." He smiled slowly and his eyes turned smoky blue. "I can promise you that more than your curiosity would have been satisfied."

She frowned. "You want to satisfy my curiosity, don't you, David?" Her mood had shifted. It wasn't a lighthearted game any longer. It was a deep emotional issue.

"What do you think? I'm a man, aren't I? And you are a very desirable woman."

His words made her feel cheap. Not any woman, surely? The woman you love. Why didn't he say it? Why didn't he tell her that he loved her? Why didn't he make it right and drive all thoughts of Justine from her mind?

"Why did you marry me?" she asked in a desperate bid to make him own to it.

"Hey, what is this?" he inquired, regarding her with a look of perplexity. "You're not blowing cold on me, are you?"

She flared back at him, "Oh, no. You can have your rights. It's what you married me for, isn't it?"

His brow furrowed in anger. "I don't know what gets into you. You can switch moods with the speed of light. But yes, if you insist, one of the reasons I married you was because I wanted you and I knew I couldn't have you any other way."

It was what she already knew, so why did she feel as though she was supporting an intolerable burden? Even keeping her eyes open was an effort, as though the desolation of her thoughts had weighted her eyelids. Her chin would have drooped too but for the cruelly tight hold of his fingers. The bite in them was reflected in his voice as an unpleasant and mocking bitterness.

"Oddly enough, I thought I was paying you a compliment in finding you desirable. I didn't know you would find it so disgusting."

Disgusting? He must know that was the last thing she found it. His other hand was on the small of her back, holding her close in its iron caress. There was nothing disgusting in the smoldering torment that teased her emotions raw, an ecstasy of feeling that was almost too painful to sustain.

"Oh, Pet, I want you, but . . ." He swallowed and his face contorted, then his expression quickly became guarded. Once again his features were cut from stone. "I will not take you against your will. Why are you holding me off?" he demanded curtly. "For heaven's sake, Petrina, why?"

She didn't want to hold him off. She wanted to be consumed by the fire. Could she help it if it would not flame for her without that vital spark? It wasn't her fault that it would not ignite for her without love. And yet she knew that if he chose to take her without love she wouldn't be able to find the will to resist. Her reasoning powers had gone. She was not even answerable to pride anymore—only desire.

"You said one of the reasons you married me," she said, holding tenaciously on to that. "And the other?"

His mouth closed around a callous laugh. "Oh, no, Pet. I'm not telling that."

"But there *was* another reason?" she persisted.

"Yes. And it's lucky for me there was. If I'd married you to have sex with you, and for no other reason, that would be my bad luck, because I haven't had it."

She faced up to his jeering look, his cruel humor, and said slowly, "You're not going to tell me?"

"You've finally got the message. If ever there comes a time when I feel inclined to tell you, it will be unnecessary, because it will mean you know."

She did know. Justine had already told her. He'd married her to throw Justine's husband off the scent so that he could keep both his job and his mistress. How could she have let David mesmerize her to the extent of forgetting that, even for a moment?

"What's it to be, Pet? Do I take you to bed or down to dinner?"

"Down to dinner," she replied haughtily, forcing back the tears that would have completed her humiliation. "I don't think I'll be able to eat anything, but I can stomach you even less."

Violence burned in his eyes. He looked livid enough to strangle her, and his hand slid down from her chin to her neck as though with that intention. His thumb found appeasement in tormenting the pulse in the hollow of her throat.

"You're hurting me," she said in protest.

"I ought to," he rasped. "You're the most perverse contradiction I've ever met. Primness and passion. Ice and fire. Stop and go. Make your mind up. One of these days you'll be shouting stop and I won't be able to. And when that happens, as it surely will if you don't get yourself sorted out, don't yell rape."

Chapter Five

The door slammed shut after him. Obviously he'd gone down to the dining room, leaving her to follow or not as she pleased.

She was glad he'd raged out by himself and that he hadn't insisted on her accompanying him. She wasn't hungry. The thought of food turned her stomach.

Although he'd removed himself physically, the room was full of his presence. His voice whispered in her brain, calling her "Pet" in cold affection, sliding his tongue torturingly over the endearment in mockery. She could still feel the shivery touch of his fingertips trailing down her upstretched arms, the burning intimacy of the hand that moved slowly down her spine to hold her body captive against his. The distinctive smell of his after-shave lingered on the air and pervaded her nostrils.

She went out onto the balcony in search of release, breathing deeply to banish his scent, hoping the gentle caress of the pleasantly cool night air would supplant the hard feel of his hands on her body and that the rushing, blissfully soothing sound of the sea could suppress the hateful sarcasm of his voice saying her name.

The sound of the sea was like light music, a harmony and discord of magical clashes and chords that relaxed only the surface of her brain and pleased without conscious effort. It did not drown out her thoughts or prevent her from sinking into the tormented depths of her mind.

She had no idea how long she sat there—she had no notion of time at all. It could have been half an hour or it could just as easily have been three hours before she went back inside and wearily began to prepare for bed.

When she looked around for her modest cotton nightgown, it was not to be found. The black nightgown, that erotic whisper of lace that Justine's goading had made her buy, had been laid out in its place. The chambermaid must have picked up her clean cotton nightgown by mistake when she collected the things to be laundered. Petrina remembered flinging her new purchase on the bed in disgust. When the maid came in later to turn down the beds, she must have assumed the nightgown was there for that purpose and had put it out for her to wear.

It was the last straw. And putting it on and seeing how transparent it was, she realized with a harsh laugh that a straw would have provided more effective cover. She didn't know why she'd even bothered to try it on because she had no intention of wearing such a tantalizing garment.

She twisted curiously in front of the mirror, shocked

and intrigued by her appearance. Even complete nakedness would not have looked so enticing. At the slightest movement, the swaying sensuality of the material emphasized a smoldering sexuality she hadn't known she possessed. The opalescent gleam of her soft curves was more than a mere invitation, it was almost a demand to be ravished. Her breasts were pure provocation; her tiny waist and slenderly curved hips acquired a sinuousness that was wanton incitement.

She hadn't realized that the bedroom had become her stage, that she was emulating the movements of a dance, or that at some point during the performance she had acquired an audience until she heard David's amused drawl.

"Do I applaud, make a grab, or contain myself for the finale?"

A wave of white-hot embarrassment rushed over her as she swung her chin up to face him in angry defiance. "There's no finale."

"No?" he queried.

"I didn't know you were there," she said a little desperately as the gleam in his eyes forced her to lower hers.

Even with her lashes glued together and her chin tucked into her throat, she could not shut out the feeling of his eyes stripping her of the flimsy concealment of her nightgown. They stalked her with the primitive passion of an animal who's been given the scent and intends to move in for the kill. The sensual exploration of his gaze was like a finger skimming her body and touching all the vulnerable, sensitive areas.

"And I thought that delightful spectacle was put on for my benefit," he drawled unpleasantly.

"You could have said something to let me know you

were there," she said in steadfast recrimination, making herself look at him.

"How could I? I was bereft of speech. It seems there's a side to my demure little Pet I had no idea existed."

He thought that she'd done it deliberately, and in fairness she knew that was how it must have looked. She had brought this shame on herself. It was ridiculous to blame the nightgown, yet in putting it on she'd cast off pride and modesty and acquired a different personality.

He had removed his tie and his jacket and was in the process of unbuttoning his shirt. "It's bedtime, Pet."

The emphasis he put on the words drained the color from her cheeks and then brought it rushing back again.

Why had she wasted time on a whimsy that was so out of character with her nature? Why, when she realized her cotton nightgown was missing, hadn't she gone straight to the drawer where she'd put her spare nightgown? Why was she wasting time thinking about it now? Why didn't she do it?

She reached the drawer; her fingernails scraped the handle. His arms came around her middle and closed over her stomach to lift her back against his body. His mouth dropped to her neck, scorching over the already highly sensitized skin.

"Please, David, no," she gasped in useless appeal.

"After all the trouble you've gone to? It would be ungallant for me not to be suitably appreciative."

He swung her around. One hand kept hold of her while the other fingered the delicate tracery of lace at her breast. She found she had to draw in her breath in quick shallow gulps. She couldn't seem to get enough air into her lungs.

"The nightgown . . . it was a mistake."

"Sure it was, Pet," he said, his finger sliding beneath the lace with a tantalizingly light touch. "A mistake. Cry about it tomorrow. Enjoy it now."

As her heart slid sideways, a genuine feeling of weakness assailed her. "David." Her voice quivered on tears as she tried to reason with him. "You can't mean to . . ." She could not go on.

His eyes passed sentence as they gloated over her in taut triumph. "Oh, but I do."

In the captivity of his loosely held arms, she knew intuitively that if she used force to escape, his hold would tighten. She didn't want that. She knew just how much her resolve would be worth if she felt the hard muscular strength of him. She knew that her resistance would melt into response. Even now, while she was still mentally holding him off, she could feel a languorous weakness creeping insidiously into her limbs.

He was accomplished in all the tricks. The one he was employing now by way of a starter was devastatingly effective. He'd put his own passion on ice, conserving himself while bringing her to heel with a playful process of light touches that were not followed up. His hands made butterfly movements over her breasts. It was torment to be touched and yet not to be touched.

His mouth played the same insouciant game, coming down on hers not in passion, but lightly, exhorting her to respond. Against her will, she found herself straining up to him. It required only a few more moments of patient restraint on his part and he could have molded her to his command. But he mistimed it. He came in too soon, before she was ready to yield to him.

The switch from light teasing to hard passion was too abrupt for her to adjust. She tensed away from the bruising demands of his mouth; she panicked as his loose hold turned into a grip of iron. She reacted to a wild, animal instinct to break free from this choking stranglehold and escape the primitive sensation of thigh against thigh, the steel domination of his hands on the small of her back. The tiny flame of terror, fanned into being by her dread of the unknown rather than revulsion, exploded into a holocaust of fear.

It wasn't until she glimpsed the expression on his face that the truth dawned on her. She knew what her struggling to get free was achieving. Of course he hadn't mistimed. This was what he wanted.

The knowledge came too late. He was sweeping her up into his arms and carrying her over to the bed. Everything she did was wrong. When she held off, she incited him; when she didn't, she incited him more.

"It's no good looking at me with those huge remonstrative eyes," he said sternly, as he not ungently lowered her onto the bed. "I warned you that if you gave me the go signal once more there'd be no going back on it."

She closed her lashes in silent despair and felt the bed give as he added his weight to it. The warmth of his body couldn't warm the root of frozen fear inside her.

The trembling in her lower lip spread to her limbs. She began to shake with violent ague. She bit hard on her lip in an attempt to regain some semblance of tranquillity and stop the spasms.

"It will be all right," he soothed. "Relax."

"I'm trying to," she stammered through quivering lips.

He held his head back and viewed her critically. "No one could be this scared. You're ill. Why didn't you tell me? How long have you been like this?"

"I guess since lunchtime." Her relief that he had

stopped was evident in her voice. "It comes and goes. I'm fine one moment and the next I feel positively ghastly."

He touched her forehead. "You're burning up. Just what have you been doing—or overdoing—today?"

"This morning I went swimming in the sea."

"And then?"

"I was wet."

"Naturally."

"And s–so I dried off in the sun." She frowned. "I knew I should have bought a sun hat *sooner* rather than *later*. Have I got sunstroke?"

"What do you expect with your fair skin and no sun hat. Throat dry?"

"Yes."

The bed creaked and lightened. "I'll get you something to drink and an extra blanket."

"I don't want an extra blanket. I'm too hot as it is. Why don't you shout at me and call me a fool for staying out too long in the sun?"

"What good would that do?"

"I'm sorry, David," she said apathetically, feeling slightly cheered that she wasn't going to be scolded.

She could remember the comfort of the drink David brought her and very little else. She couldn't remember his getting back into bed with her. She didn't know a thing until she woke next morning to find him there beside her.

It was a very strange, not at all unpleasant sensation to realise she'd shared her bed with a man, with this man.

She stole a shy look at his undeniably handsome profile. Once his even breathing had assured her he was not awake, she leaned up on her elbow to see him better. His rumpled hair, which revealed a tendency to curl, wasn't at all in keeping with his urbane, coldly professional facade. He had shed several years in sleep and not only did he look less formidable, but to see him now one could almost be forgiven for thinking he was a soft touch. Sleep had robbed his mouth of scorn and had given him back the vulnerable look he'd had as a boy. His eyelids were closed over the cynicism that lurked so near the surface in his blue eyes, and the tender sweep of his eyelashes on his deeply suntanned face added a touch of unconscious sensuality. He was on his back with one arm slung at a nonchalant angle over his head.

He moved, turning slightly in her direction, but his lashes remained firmly closed and she was convinced he had stirred in his sleep. So she released her held breath and continued to enjoy him with her eyes.

Considering that his job employed more brain power than brawn he was very powerfully built. He had strong, muscular shoulders and a lean torso with ribs covered only by strong, gleaming muscles and deeply tanned skin. The bedclothes barely covered his midriff and she had a strong suspicion that he wasn't wearing anything apart from the gold chain around his neck. A medallion was suspended from the finely chased links and rested in the dark hairs on his chest.

She was just thinking that such a frank stare would not be possible if he were awake and making a reciprocal appraisal, when his eyes opened. He sat up and the bed clothes shifted, confirming her suspicion about his nakedness. But that wasn't the sum total of her consternation. The devil gleam in his eye and the peculiar lift of his mouth provided advance warning that he'd been awake for some moments. She blushed before he uttered a word.

"Well, what's the verdict? Do I pass?"

"You . . . I thought you were asleep," she said, averting her eyes.

"Did you?" he said, as his eyes laughed lazily over her face. A sinewy muscle rippled against her neck as he reached to take a handful of her hair as leverage and twisted her face around to his. "Just in case you have any plans that don't coincide with mine, like leaping out of bed."

"It's what I usually do when I wake up," she said, her demure voice at variance with her alerted senses. A tingling exhilaration raced through her body, paced by a strange ache. The last thing she wanted to do was leap out of bed. She wanted to snuggle down into bed, close beside him.

She found herself doing this, not exactly following her inclinations but responding to the tugging pain in her scalp as his fingers tightened more forcefully in the tangled strands of her hair to bring her down.

"And how do you feel this morning, Mrs. Palmer?"

"I'm better."

His lips moved over her shoulder to her throat, seducing the arched column of her neck with kisses, tormenting the corner of her mouth, tasting her earlobe. The intensity of feeling built up, and the ague was back.

The smile on his mouth was swallowed in a groan of concern for her and dismay for himself. "You're shaking. Pet, please don't have a relapse on me."

"I'm not ill now. I'm what you first thought I was when I started shaking last night."

"Scared?" he puzzled.

"M'm."

"Don't be, my Pet."

He smooth-talked her all the way; his fingers caressed and persuaded with an understanding and sensitivity that took every part of her into his protection and demanded, and got, her complete trust. Her heart filled with more love for him than she had thought possible and she gave herself to him in awesome adoration at his gentleness. His approach was casual, as if he knew her tormented senses could not take too much at once. In this way she barely realized the moment of trauma had passed until the bliss was upon her, drawing her into its enthralling grip.

She lay in his arms, hugging to her that unforgettable, perfect moment, that magical exaltation. The surprise and beauty of it brought tears to her eyes. David kissed them away, tender in his concern, fearful they were tears of pain and not jewels of happiness.

Her fingers were tightly entwined around his neck. Even when he no longer possessed her, she still clung to him, reluctant to drag herself away, savoring the sweetness of the afterglow. She knew that Justine had had no place in his thoughts that morning, and all her fears of the other woman were quickly fading before the glow in David's eyes.

"Well?" he said, looking deeply into her eyes in a way that suggested he'd had a few surprises himself.

She had taken no conscious initiative, her fingers had made no love play, but as his body had cherished her inexperience, hers had drawn deeply on its instincts to harmonize with his in artless simplicity.

"Was it so obvious it was my first time?" she asked, feeling suddenly very shy.

"What an ingenue you are," he said in mocking delight as though the thought pleased him.

"That doesn't answer my question."

"Yes, it was obvious."

"But not at first? It was something you found out as you went along?"

"Yes." He grinned. "You still haven't told me what you thought of it."

"It was all right, I suppose. The actual thing rarely lives up to the expectation," she said wickedly, paying him back for not knowing she was a virgin.

His reply was as swift as it was predictable. "That was just a rehearsal." One eyebrow arched. "We'll get better, but we'll have to practice every spare moment we can."

"I was joking!" she gasped.

"I wasn't." He cupped her face in his hands and crushed her mouth under his. "And now, very reluctantly, I must get up. I've a full day's work facing me."

"Must you work today?"

He groaned. "I must." He lifted a strand of her hair and let its silkiness slide through his fingers. His face fell into an expression that she found impossible to read. "I've been thinking over what you said yesterday. You accused me of not telling you anything and deliberately shutting you out of my working life. How would you like to be included for a change?"

"I'd like that," she said expectantly.

"This morning I'm going to inspect a castle. I take it you want to come with me?"

"A castle?" she said, her imagination soaring. "A *real* castle. Can I honestly come?"

"I've said so, haven't I?" he said on an abrupt and repressive change of tone. "Bear in mind that this is Chimera. Nothing is real on Chimera. It is, most fittingly, a mock castle. Recently built to look centuries old, because people expect to find a castle on an island and will shell out good money for a night, or a weekend even, of medieval entertainment."

"Just a holiday attraction," she said, making no

attempt to hide her disappointment. "Another way of milking the tourist."

"There you go again. And you wonder why I don't tell you anything. I should have my head examined for bothering."

She couldn't believe how quickly the tender warmth they had shared until just a moment ago had gone, to be replaced by his usual iciness.

Ungraciously following his lead, she shrugged indifferently. "Even visiting a mock castle will be better than hanging around here all day."

If she'd probed she would have found lurking at the back of her mind the ungerminated seed of thought that it was her own disdainful opinion of the way he conducted himself in business that had brought him to swift and angry retaliation. She told herself he was reverting to type and that he was arrogant and insensitive by nature, and ignored the possibility that he could well be driven to hit out in blind frustration by the unyielding quality of her attitude.

She was tempted to add to his annoyance by taking a long time over getting ready and so delay the early start he claimed he was anxious to make. But she thought twice about that, and her second thought convinced her she could be the loser. He was astute enough to figure out her tactics, and brutal enough to sweep her out of the hotel without breakfast. As she had already been cheated out of dinner last night, she was hungrier than usual.

On inspiration, instead of the rolls and preserves that would have sufficed, she ordered a full English breakfast, and took pleasure in the fact that David occupied the time while it was being cooked by drumming his fingers on the table.

She overdid the ordering, because such a huge

breakfast did not meet with her stomach's approval, and had to struggle gamely through two eggs, bacon, sausages, and two saucer-large slices of fried tomato, while he looked on with an "I-should-say-that-evens-the-score" smirk on his mouth.

It was a small consolation that they had the breakfast table to themselves. The other places had been cleared away, so presumably Ginny and Bob had already eaten.

David had made no mention of Ginny going with them and so Petrina was surprised to see the tall, skinny blond installed in the Land Rover that was waiting for them at the front of the hotel.

This morning Ginny wore pale sand-colored trousers and a checked cotton overshirt that, because of its fine material and aided by Ginny's omission to fasten the buttons, all but the one in line with her bra, revealed more than it concealed although, with her statistics, there wasn't all that much to reveal. It was difficult to pinpoint what made Ginny attractive. Her looks didn't fit into any of the accepted categories. She wasn't aloof and elegant, and she wasn't romantically pretty. Her keynote was more subtle and less easy to define. Her vitality would play an important part, and that enviable air of self-assurance. Though Petrina didn't think that Ginny was as assured as she tried to make out.

She hoped her own choice, a casual shirtwaist dress that had looked fine in her bedroom mirror, would pass muster. It was in soft companion colors of blues and greens, shading from one to the other with no definite pattern. She had left the top two buttons fashionably open to reveal her throat. She fingered the third button absentmindedly, caught David's wicked glance, and thought better of it.

In lieu of apology for keeping her waiting, David told Ginny she looked very spruce. Ginny's beaming smile forgave him, and, to her dismay, Petrina found she had to avert her eyes. She knew she was being unreasonable and foolish about this, and furthermore it was unworthy of her, but she was jealous of the camaraderie David and Ginny shared. She told herself sternly that she should be grateful her husband had found such a loyal and seemingly efficient secretary to back him up in his difficult job, and she was sure now that there was nothing between them, but still she envied the bond they shared, a bond that she and David might never have.

This brought a strange thought to mind. Ginny was on the spot. She was a likeable person and extremely easy going. She had proved this by not objecting to being the butt of Bob's humor when they'd shared a breakfast table. And, in its own way, her boyish sex appeal was quite fetching. If David had needed to produce a decoy to allay Geoffrey Hyland's suspicions and so safeguard his job, why hadn't he chosen Ginny?

A tiny frown etched itself between her fine brows at a possible conclusion to be drawn from this. Perhaps it was harder to find a loyal secretary than it was to find a wife. Any presentable young woman would fit this latter role, whereas a secretary of Ginny's worth might be difficult to come by. Petrina was sorry she had ever even considered the question.

Chapter Six

The road followed a confusing, winding course, in keeping with her thoughts. She was certain she hadn't been just any woman in David's arms a short while ago. It had been special to her, and she had been so sure it had been special to him. Could he have been like that with her and still long for Justine? She'd given her heart when she'd given her body. He'd been tender with both of them, as if he recognized the gift of her love and was happy to accept it. Perhaps he was. It didn't mean that he had to reciprocate it, or that his affair with Justine had come to an end.

With grim determination she dropped her thoughts and concentrated on the scenery. For the most part the road traveled along the coastline, but occasionally it plunged inland to climb through dark green forests, where tall, tightly packed trees screened hidden places and lurking dangers—some real, others the menacing creations of the imagination. They left the umbrellalike gloom behind and she gleaned what dubious solace she could from keeping track of the hairpin bends and she trusted her stomach not to disgrace her as her eyes dipped dizzily down a sheer cliff face to the sparkling innocence of the turquoise sea.

"A considerable amount of fortifying and rebuilding is being carried out to bring the road up to the required safety standards before we can trundle up the coachloads of tourists," David explained.

She had seen the evidence of this because they had already passed several gangs of workmen employed in the task. Once he stopped the Land Rover and got out to have a word with the workmen. He seemed concerned because that particular stretch wasn't being completed quickly enough. At the same time, she wondered if he'd sensed her queasiness and was teasing her when he said the tourists would come along this route. The road seemed much too narrow ever to accommodate a coach.

"There is a better way," Ginny said, apparently by chance, because Petrina didn't think she was interpreting her thoughts.

"A better way?" David queried thoughtfully. "Progress demanded the building of a less hazardous, more direct road, if that's what you mean."

With a strange reversal of thought, Petrina realized that David was not taking a dig at her, but expressing a side of himself that his brisk business mind usually kept well hidden. Did he come down on the side of progress by determination and not natural inclination?

Suddenly the brave little road was no longer a threat to safety and the density of the trees was not as menacing. Her spirits lifted on the sparkling beauty of the day. It was an appropriate moment to catch her first glimpse of the castle.

It might have been built only recently as a money-making project, a setting deliberately contrived for medieval banquets and jousting tournaments and anything else they might dream up to tempt the tourist to open up his wallet, but seen with the dazzle of the sun in her eyes—she still hadn't bought sunglasses and the protective brim of her sun hat wasn't pulled far enough down—it was like a vision from ancient legend.

Stepping down from the Land Rover to the rough ground, she appreciated David's steadying hand, and not only for the assistance it provided. She wished that Ginny weren't efficiently getting her notebook out and that David didn't have to work. If only she could keep her fingers tightly curled in his and they could ignore Ginny and wander off by themselves.

Instead, she was the one left on her own while David barked out instructions to the workmen and Ginny jotted down notes when required.

A man who looked a bit better dressed than the majority of the workmen and was obviously in charge approached David. Some query in the main hall required David's attention. As the two men crossed the drawbridge and disappeared beyond the stout, studded wooden door, Petrina found herself unexpectedly alone with Ginny.

The shirt, she noticed, was now demurely buttoned up, but not Ginny's mouth. "It's not that your husband is a prude, it's just that he prefers the men to keep their eyes on their work." Her laugh was slightly rueful. "Not that I'm much of a distracting influence; I'm just one of the guys." Ginny wasn't fishing for compliments but she had something on her mind, and Petrina wasn't surprised to hear her say abruptly, "I believe in being frank, don't you?"

"Every time."

"Good. You might have noticed that I'm excessively loyal to your husband."

"It is rather obvious."

"You're looking at all the angles and are wondering why. Yes?"

"I'll go along with that."

"What answer have you come up with?"

"The one with the least complications. Respect isn't given, it's earned. Worker and boss must be compatible. So—you must respect David, find him fair-minded and good to work for, even though others might not see him in that way?" Petrina suggested tentatively.

Ginny's nod was emphatic. "He's been good to me and mine. I know he has his share of critics, but then people who make their mark in the world always will have. Some say he's got his eye on the main chance and that he never does anything for anybody unless there's something in it for him. In a way, I suppose that's true. My own mother is a perfect example. Do you know what he did for her?"

"No. Tell me," Petrina encouraged.

"During a rehousing program she was pushed into a high-rise apartment. She hated it. She was a sick woman to start with and the feeling of being trapped didn't help her condition. David got her out. He paid for her to go to a nursing home by the sea and, as soon as she was feeling up to it, he found a charming little house for her. He knew what he was doing when he bought it; it was on a site that was ripe for development. My mother had a blood disorder; she had no chance of recovering. When she died, David sold the house and made a bundle. I don't care if he did make a handsome profit by his good deed. My mother was happy in that little house, and that's all that matters to me."

"I'm sorry about your mother, Ginny," Petrina sympathized. "I lost my mother when I was a little girl."

"You'll know what it's all about then," Ginny said, savagely kicking at a stone and sending up a swirl of dust. "I had to tell you this to set you straight. I would like us to be friends, and—well—you've been giving me some rather searching looks."

"I'm sorry. You're very perceptive, Ginny."

"It doesn't pay not to be." Now it was Ginny's turn to send her the searching look. "You should mark that."

"Thanks. I will." She hesitated before going on. Ginny was warning her to keep her eyes open so she obviously *knew*. Deciding she had nothing to lose and perhaps something to gain, she plunged on recklessly, "You know about Justine, don't you, Ginny?"

Ginny's breath sucked in. "I didn't think you'd know—not so soon."

"Perhaps I should modify that," Petrina said, underplaying her suspicions to gain Ginny's information. "I think there might have been something going on between my husband and Justine."

Ginny looked shattered. "I only meant to put you on your guard. I take no pleasure in getting involved, but I guess I brought it on myself at that. So—here goes. I'm sure David only befriended Justine Hyland in the first place for her husband's sake, but she might not have seen it that way. The signs are that she hasn't. She's become very possessive about David just lately. It must have been a dreadful shock to her when he came back and brought you with him. I've got an awful feeling she's not going to take it mildly and I think you might have to bear the brunt of her vindictive tongue."

She wondered what Ginny would say if she told her she had already been treated, at considerable length, to Justine's vituperation. No, she couldn't tell Ginny about that. It was much too personal. Instead, she said, "Where is Justine's husband?"

"He comes and goes. His various business commitments require him to travel a good deal."

"Why doesn't Justine go with him? Why does she stay here?"

The brown eyes were wary. "I'm not in her confidence. Perhaps she just likes it here."

"You mean, perhaps she likes being near David. What kind of man is Geoffrey Hyland?"

"A very wealthy one," Ginny replied drily. "Without the weight of his money all this"—she waved her hands expansively to cover the castle and the new direct road that had been built—"couldn't have been accomplished for ages."

Petrina wasn't surprised to have her surmise confirmed that Geoffrey Hyland was David's boss.

Meanwhile, Ginny was suffering remorse. "Me and my big mouth. David would skin me if he knew."

"David won't know. Cheer up, Ginny, you deserve a medal for the discretion of your answers. You haven't been disloyal to David; I dragged it out of you."

Shortly after that, David rejoined them. He sneaked up behind Petrina and slid his hands around her waist. After that enlightening talk with Ginny, she didn't feel very affectionate toward him, but she submitted to being squeezed because the place was too public for her to put up a struggle.

By that strange one-way telepathic intelligence he had somehow rigged up in his favor, he was immediately plugged into her mental rejection and had his own way of dealing with it. On the way back to the Land Rover she got the cold shoulder. It was Ginny's shoulder that received the warmth of his arm casually slung around it as he pointedly began to tell her about a work matter the morning had turned up. It was some moments before his eyes lifted from Ginny's face to slide coolly back to Petrina. The message was clear. If she got that sort of notion she would be the loser, since he could find plenty to interest himself in his job.

Blast his arrogance! She would not be brought to heel like that. She resisted the childish impulse to stamp her foot in frustration and did something even more stupid. She stalked on ahead, and then had a fuming wait by the Land Rover as David dawdled along, keeping Ginny with him by keeping his arm draped over her, making no effort to catch up to Petrina.

She should have been with them, actively interested in what they were saying. She had accused David of shutting her out of his working life—this time she had shut herself out.

Back at the hotel, David suggested they go up to their own quarters for a quick wash and general freshen up, and meet again for lunch. Ginny had only just sauntered away when Bob stopped them.

"Can you spare a moment, David?" He apologized to Petrina. "I'm sorry, Trina, you must be dead sick of us."

"Not you, Bob," she said with specific meaning.

"The demands of the job then. You're a very understanding woman. May I also say how charming you look?"

"You certainly may." After the morning's frustrations, Bob's brash charm was like a soothing balm to her wounded pride. When she looked at David she saw he was frowning heavily.

His voice was harsh as he said, "Go on up, Petrina. I'll keep this short."

She went up, leaving them to their talk, grateful to have this time to herself. It wouldn't be long enough for her to take a shower if they were to keep David's promise to meet Ginny for lunch. She removed her dress and made do with a quick splash to her arms and face.

She was contemplating her abandoned dress when David came in. His eyes flicked over her as she stood there in her slip. His expression surprised her. The tingling fire-force of his emotions was visible in every strained nerve. She had long since gauged him to be a man very much in control of himself, and it was startling to think that he might be aroused at coming in on her like this.

More in confusion than seeking advice, she said, "I suppose I ought to find another dress to change into. I'm afraid my choice is limited though."

His brow was down. "Is that what's eating you?" In three strides he was by her side. "Do you feel cheated? I said you would. No time to buy a trousseau. No engagement ring. No honeymoon."

She did feel cheated, but not because of a few pretty dresses or not being given an engagement ring. Not even about the honeymoon. A honeymoon wasn't a romantic place—it was two people in love, just being together. She couldn't even be certain she was getting a raw deal. It would be unfair to condemn David for what he'd been to Justine before and she hadn't expected him to say, "Look, I had an affair with this woman but it's over now." If it *was* over. Wasn't that her fear, the crux of her unrest?

David's glance narrowed on her face, as though trying to read the thoughts whipping her expression into a state of turbulence. He picked up her hand. "I hardly dare touch you. I've got to keep it light, otherwise we won't be going down to lunch."

"I've no intention of skipping lunch," she said haughtily.

"No?" he queried tantalizingly.

In a not very steady voice she said, "Ginny will be waiting downstairs."

His brief shrug dismissed Ginny. His eyes were shuttered to all but one thing. Had there been no conflict between them, no disturbing issues to confuse her mind, she would have thought: his love. But there were conflict and other issues, so—his physical need of her, his desire. Its compelling force tormented the air she was breathing and ground his voice down to a husky whisper.

"You shall have your honeymoon. Soon. I promise. And I'll buy you a ring in the not too distant future. What is your choice? Diamonds, following tradition? Sapphires? Rubies? Emeralds?"

She was hurting too much to be cajoled for the price of a trinket, however expensive. "You don't have to promise me goodies, David. I'm your wife."

"I could pick something very unpleasant out of that. But I won't; I don't want to argue with you."

With a teasing flicker of her lashes, half afraid of the violence she might provoke, she said, "Of course, master. We must always do what you want to do. You don't want to argue. Argument ended."

"It doesn't sound that way to me. It seems to have only just begun, although I don't know what started it. I do know I'm losing patience with you."

One hand still held hers, the other was by his side,

but not for long. Anticipation of being swept into his arms held her on dagger points, impaling her nerve ends, her breath. It was almost a relief when the tormenting wait ended and she felt herself being crushed against his chest.

Would she always experience this jolt of surprise? Before marrying David, she had never realized what a delicious sensation it was to be touched. Tiny buds of excitement seemed to burst just beneath the surface of her skin as his caressing fingers compelled a craving in her that matched his own. Her traitorous body was hungry for him, but her mind refused to succumb. Her restraint turned the pleasure pulses he had aroused into points of pain.

She clenched her fingers, trying to support her determination with movement, but instead of hitting wildly at nothing, her knuckles grazed down his hips. The unexpected contact uncurled her hands; they turned and flattened against his thighs. The muscular hardness of his body soaked the strength out of her fingers. It took barely two weakening seconds for her arms to lift and slide around his neck where twining finger met twining finger. "The ring of seduction," he called it. But there was no seduction mirrored in her eyes, only the loving passion she felt for him.

Her hands slid down to trace, through his shirt, the line of his spine and the outlines of his strongly muscled chest. Almost surprised by her willing acquiescence, he trailed his fingers lightly over her breasts and touched his lips to the hollow at the base of her throat. His eyes grew smoky with passion as he led her gently to the bed.

He drew her down beside him and pushed aside the straps of her slip, dropping the thin cloth barrier from her breasts, then buried his face in the hollow between them before letting his tongue trace sensuously over their rosy tips. Petrina made a small sound of pleasure as she pressed him closer, her body arching against the muscular length of his. That he desired her was evident in his husky breathing and the pounding of his heart, and when at last she gave herself completely to him, it was in loving submission.

Some time later, he said, "Sorry to sound repetitive, darling, but I must drag myself away. I have work to do."

She bit back a plaintive "Must you?" and said, "What about your lunch?"

"I'll get something and eat it as I go along."

"Go along where?"

"I'm not very happy about one stretch of the road we went along this morning."

"Only one stretch? I wasn't very happy about most of it."

His head went to one side. "In case you hadn't noticed, there's a storm brewing."

Now he came to mention it, she had wondered at the peculiar yellow brightness of the sky and the stillness of the air.

"It's forecast to hit us by tomorrow morning. Just to be on the safe side, I've decided to direct the entire work force to that one piece of road. I don't want all that effort to be washed away." He dropped a kiss on the end of her nose. "I'll get a lunch tray sent up for you."

"You won't," she protested. "I'm going down to the dining room."

He looked at his watch. "It closed five minutes ago."

"Oh, dear! What will the staff think? And Ginny? We were supposed to be joining her!"

His eyes glinted wickedly. "Ginny is very understanding. Her romantic heart will be making a big sighing 'Aaah'. The staff is more likely to be saying, 'That terrible Señor Palmer can't keep his hands off his little *esposa* and gets her into bed at every possible moment'."

"Thank you very much," she said, blushing rosily, scrambling to make herself look presentable.

She was sitting on the balcony when the waiter arrived with her lunch tray. It all looked delicious. Fillet of hake in a spicy tomato sauce with slivers of lightly toasted almonds, a cold meat salad, and fruit. There was also a small bottle of white wine.

As soon as the shops were open again after siesta, she intended to do some shopping. As well as sunglasses and protective cream, she also required soothing lotion for her lobster-red shoulders and a tender bit at the top of her right thigh, earned from her ill-fated drying off in the sun yesterday. She must also remember to buy a postcard to send to Uncle Richard.

On stepping out of the elevator she bumped into the one person she most wanted to avoid: Justine Hyland.

"Hello," she said hollowly.

"Hi!" Justine responded in an overfriendly tone. "All set for the barbecue tonight?"

"Barbecue?"

"On the beach, if the weather holds. Didn't David tell you?"

"No," she said, unwisely letting her irritation show. It was just that he never seemed to tell her anything. She had to find out everything the hard way.

"Perhaps he didn't think you'd fancy it," Justine suggested slyly.

"Well, he's wrong. Because I do."

"Splendid. He makes a wonderful dancing partner. See you there!"

"You can count on it." And we'll see whose dancing partner he is, she thought. "What's the dress?"

"Anything, as long as it's casual."

She mentally plundered her wardrobe and added another item to her shopping list: something special to wear this evening.

The sunglasses, the various lotions, a postcard, and stationery were no trouble to acquire. The something special to wear took rather longer to be selected. She had an idea what Justine meant by "casual" and she wasn't going to be caught out. The final choice rested between a revealing slinky black dress and a pair of tight-fitting white trousers, which she teamed with a plain black top that was so skimpy it was nearly a miss, but scored a hit when she put it on. The trousers and top were the less daring of the two, so she decided on those.

Back at the hotel, settled in her favorite chair on her balcony, she wrote both the postcard and a letter to Uncle Robert. The postcard showed an aerial view of the island with a border of scenic pictures. There was one bay in particular that captured her heart, but she had no idea just where on the island it was. The letter paper gave more space for writing.

She put down her pen and sat back, thinking how dramatically her life had changed in the span of a few days. The postcard of the island was responsible for triggering nostalgia. In particular, the tiny bay that was the unspoiled image of her father's dream of Chimera caught her eye. What would he think if he could see how cruelly his dream had been misused? Everything that had been accomplished was the exact opposite of what he had set out to create.

Big money had come in to achieve the violation. She had an idea stirring in her mind that David was more than a key man employed to do a responsible job. She thought it possible that he'd invested some of his own money in the project and was entitled to a say in the way things were conducted. But there was a major shareholder who had the final word. In her mind he had always been The Opportunist or The Profiteer. Now she had another name to link with those two: Geoffrey Hyland.

What was he like? Not the kind of man who would meet with her approval, she feared. She could never like him for what he'd done to Chimera, for destroying her father's dream. David condemned her attitude. A tiny part of her knew that he was right and she was being unreasonable. Only a fool would have followed her father's exact plan and not been guided by his mistakes. Geoffrey Hyland was neither a fool nor a philanthropist. By all accounts he was a hard-headed businessman who had come in to bail her father out, not out of the goodness of his heart, but to make a profit.

She was glad now that when her father came out of exile she'd abandoned her own plans of getting a job, or embarking on some kind of training to equip her to get a job, to keep house for him. Those two years had been good. There hadn't been any money to spare, because her father had failed to climb back onto the bandwagon of success, but they'd reached a better understanding, grown closer.

On his death, David had unexpectedly come to rescue her from the bad publicity raked up by a ghoulish press. And here she was.

Chapter Seven

Petrina was ready for the barbecue and still David hadn't returned. When he did, she half wished she wasn't so obviously ready to go out. It wasn't just the flicker of annoyance on his face when he took in her appearance and made the correct interpretation, but the tiredness that showed around his eyes and mouth and seemed to have eaten up his normal vitality. Even the usual sardonic twinkle was absent from his eye. The twist of sadness in her stomach took her by surprise because she would never have thought that roguish gleam was something she'd yearn to see. Difficult as it was to believe, it was easier on her emotions to be plagued by him than to feel compassion for him.

"I heard about the beach barbecue," she explained. "I thought it might be fun."

She felt quilty now about whimpering on about being

neglected. He worked too hard, against pressures she knew nothing about and a clock that remained steadfastly just a bit ahead. She had been an unwanted complication, and instead of being grateful that he was fitting her in she had been fiercely resentful, too engrossed in herself to spare a moment of wifely concern for him.

"Who told you about the barbecue?"

"Justine," she said, puzzled by his angry tone.

"I'd guessed—Bob," he said more amenably.

Had the idea of going to the barbecue become more attractive because Justine was behind it?

"If you're too tired . . . ?" she began tentatively.

"I'll feel better when I've had a shower."

"I don't mind. I'd just as soon have a quiet meal and an early night."

"I've told you I'll be all right," he said grittily. "Why do you have to be so perverse? If I'd said I was too tired, you'd have sulked."

Her eyes blazed into anger. "I do not sulk. I might lash out in temper and even throw things, but I never sink into crabby silence, which is what I presume you mean by sulking. And it's insulting of you to suggest I do."

The faintest of smiles was tempted to his mouth. "You're right, I'm wrong. I apologize. Now stop arguing. If you don't, then I'll stop you arguing and we'll have that early night. But I promise you it won't be restful."

His eyes caught hers and she held her breath. She was incapable of releasing it until that predatory gleam, only lightly restrained, finished stalking her. She escaped the shackles of one hold only to be seized by another. As his eyes let her go his strong fingers bound her wrists and pulled her forward into his arms.

"Which will please you most," he said roughly against her cheek, "the barbecue or bed?"

"The barbecue," she said in a whisper.

Her release came too soon. "The barbecue it is. Pour me a drink, Pet, while I'm showering."

She went over to the cart containing an assortment of bottles and glasses. She said, with a touch of mischief of her own, "What would you like? No, don't tell me, let me guess. Lemonade? Orangeade? Ginger Ale?"

"The last one sounds all right. Dry Ginger Ale. Oh, and a generous measure of whisky."

She crossed her fingers and hoped this lighter mood would prevail. In combat with David she used herself up and she wanted to keep something in reserve, in case Justine had anything in store for her. It was bad enough fighting David; the prospect of fighting *for* him was not one she viewed with confidence. The new outfit had not provided the prop she thought it would despite, or perhaps *because* of, the prolonged inspection his eyes had given it.

When he appeared again, she found herself running her glance over his choice of attire with appreciation and a jolt of surprise. He, too, had opted for a change of image. In faded and obviously well-worn slacks that were an indiscriminate color between blue and grey and a dark red sweat shirt with a striped red-and-black scarf around his throat, he looked more like a beachcomber than a shrewd man of business. No, he looked less civilized than a beachcomber. A more barbaric character altogether. Yes, that was it, a pirate.

He approached her with a slow stride, even though his shower had done the revitalizing trick. His eyes strolled over her, the stubborn tilt of her chin, along her shoulder and down to the curve of her thigh, gently emphasized by the fit of her trousers. His finger trailed down accordingly, but instead of finishing the course it stayed in the shadowed hollow between her breasts.

"I don't care for my wife to show this much cleavage."

At first she thought it was a joke, but then she saw he was deadly serious.

"I went to a lot of trouble to select this outfit. I'm not changing into something else."

"I'm not asking you to. But if I were, you'd change. I'm warning you. Just because you're dressed like a tart, don't act like one."

Her frustration and hurt wanted an outlet. She was afraid she would either strike him or burst into tears. The one would have been ineffective, the other humiliating, so she only turned away from him with a painful, sinking feeling.

The air conditioning of the hotel was something that was taken for granted, barely noticed even until it was left behind. Walking out into the oppressively warm evening, she perceived that the curious yellow light of the day had plunged into an even stranger honey glow.

"Will the rain hold off for the barbecue?" she asked.

"No," David prophesied grimly. "Before the night's out we'll all be running for cover."

What thoughts were going on behind that daunting frown? Trying to probe the puzzle of his funny mood, she asked, "Is it that stretch of road you were concerned about earlier?"

"No. I did what I set out to do. It should hold up as well as anywhere."

She had supplied the opening. He obviously didn't want to tell her what was troubling him, so she let it drop.

A trail of people in antlike formation marked the route to the beach. The women stood out like a sprinkling of lotus petals in their pretty dresses or pants outfits, and she didn't feel at all outrageous in her choice.

The beach was already beginning to look quite crowded and the convivial atmosphere was infectious. Her nose tingled at the scent of wood smoke and roasted suckling pig; her blood danced to the music supplied by three *gitanos,* authentic Spanish gypsies in traditional costume.

A small welcome-to-the-party glass was put in her hand. She tipped it to her lips and drank fire. Her smarting eyes latched on to David's taunting grin.

"You could have warned me, you beast," she said between gasps and splutters.

He took her hand and guided her to a vacant spot at one of the long tables that had been set up, temptingly arrayed with bowls containing crusty hunks of bread that smelled oven fresh, green salad, bottles of red and white wine, and pitchers of sangria afloat with fruit.

As the tables filled up, more bowls appeared, chunky with potatoes, and immense platters of chicken and suckling pig. Everything was refillable—as soon as the level of anything dropped, it was heaped up again, and the empty bottles of wine and pitchers of sangria were whisked away and replaced with new ones.

"Room for one more?"

Petrina's head jerked around to see Justine's sweetly smiling face fixed on David. She gulped. Her gaze flitted between David and Justine, assessing Justine's appearance, wanting to imprint on her mind David's reaction to his former lover in her presence. He edged nearer to her, but only to make room for Justine to sit next to him on his other side. His blank expression told her nothing she didn't already know—that he was adept at hiding his feelings.

Justine's black hair was worn piled high. She wore a heavy Aztec necklace that made her throat look even more fragile than usual, emphasizing her collarbone and drawing the eyes down to the seductive cling of her black dress of shimmering satin. Was this casual? It was so tight she might have been poured into it. The sheen of the material gave her thigh a gentle curve and showed up the slightest movement of stomach muscle. Only someone as snake-supple as Justine could have got away with such a highlighting effect; on her it was the most sensational thing Petrina had ever seen.

She was not unhappy to have her thoughts distracted by the ceremony of serving the punch. Huge vats were set alight and the potent liquid was ladled into glasses. She caught a glimpse of Ginny, who was seated a few tables away, a new superlook Ginny in a green dress, her blond hair free of the usual brown ribbon, falling in a silky flick to her shoulders.

When the dancing began, she saw that the majority of the women were kicking off their sandals and dancing barefoot. She followed suit.

Taking her into his arms, David looked down at her diminished height and said, "The falsehoods you women practice."

"High heels are my only falsehood," she asserted.

"Who should know that but I?" he said, crushing her more fiercely to his body.

The wine had affected her tongue. "That would be telling."

"There's nothing to tell. I know."

"Really?" His laugh grated on her nerves, goading

her to add, "You know you were the first man to make love to me properly, I'll grant you that. But you can't know how many times I've been tempted before."

"You knew your destiny at an early age. I spoiled you for other men."

"That's an arrogant remark. Do you think yourself so superior that I can't find other men attractive?"

"You'd better not."

"But you find other women attractive."

"That's different."

"How is it? You don't own me and you can't dictate how I feel. I'm an independent person. I'm my own woman."

"You are my wife. You can only be as independent as I allow you to be."

"That is the most biased male viewpoint I've ever heard."

It wasn't even as though it was worth arguing about. She didn't want to be independent of him and she knew she could never become emotionally involved with anyone else. She loved him and he didn't have to force his mastery over her. But set against this was the driving force of her deeply hurt pride. She could not forget that he had told her she looked like a tart. If that weren't bad enough, he'd carried the insult a step further by warning her not to act like one. She wouldn't even know how, although doubtless she could get a few pointers by watching Justine.

She had to hit back and she did so by using his method, adapting his words to fit. "Just because you've adopted the clothes of a pirate it doesn't mean you have to get into the skin of the character."

"Touché," he said, and the quality of his slow-to-form smile made her almost hate him. The unreal honey dusk etched his features into a malevolent mask. He was like a stranger to her.

"I don't want to dance anymore," she said. It was a weary admission because it meant rejoining Justine. She wished Ginny and Bob were sitting at their table. Their cross quips would have gone a long way toward easing the atmosphere. It occurred to her that although she had spotted Ginny, she hadn't yet seen Bob. "Where's Bob? Have you seen him anywhere?"

David's answering tone of voice and the expression on his face baffled her. "No," he said in bitterness. "He's sure to turn up. Your efforts won't have been in vain."

Efforts? What he meant was beyond her.

As they walked away from the circle of dancers, his fingers crushed into her waist with savage deliberation, as if he didn't know his own strength or his power to hurt. It was the kind of cruelty that leaves the bloom on the skin, but bruises the heart.

He asked Justine for the next dance. It would have been ungallant of him not to, but Petrina watched the dark-haired beauty go into his arms with a hollow feeling deep in her stomach. Partners changed with the tempo of the music. But Justine's head was still in line with the flutter of David's red-and-black scarf. The total blackness of Justine's dress was relieved by her scarlet fingernails, predatory claws clinging to the darker red of David's shirt.

At the end of the dance, although she looked everywhere, there was no sign of David. Inevitably, she couldn't spot Justine anywhere either.

A hand touched her elbow. Her face leaped around.

"Sorry to disappoint you. It's only me." The tone of voice matched her expression.

"Hello, Bob. I was wondering where you'd got to."

"I came late. Your table seemed to have a full complement of people, so rather than crush in I found a place elsewhere. I wish somebody's face would light up for me as yours did just now."

"How do you know my face wasn't lighting up for you?"

"Because people, meaning females of course, don't think of me in that way. They might say, 'Good old Bob,' but their knees never buckle."

"Anybody else but you, Bob, and I'd think they were fishing."

She put her head on one side and perhaps looked at him for the first time. Not as a valuable part of her husband's team, but as a man. He had a powerful body, slightly overweight, but he had the height to carry it. He was younger than David. She gauged his age to be twenty-eight or nine. His hair was fair to sandy and he had an open, genial face. She didn't know why he was running himself down because she thought he was quite attractive. When you get to know the character behind a face, personality and looks become indivisible, but she didn't think her opinion was guided too much by her liking for the man, although it must be influenced by it to some extent.

She would never forget Bob's kindness to her when she was in torment, wondering where David had spent their wedding night. Bob hadn't known how to tell her. He'd been red-faced with embarrassment and it must have stretched his loyalty to David, but he'd overcome his scruples and his awkwardness to let her know that her husband had used the spare bed in his room. For as long as she lived, she would love Bob for that.

She touched his hand, conveying her liking for him,

not pausing to consider the folly of such an action. "You're selling yourself short, Bob. I think you're a very attractive, wonderful man."

She said it to boost his ego, make him put a value on himself, because if he didn't put a value on himself, no one else would. Only Bob himself could knock down the 'Good old Bob' image that he didn't much like. That was only one very desirable facet to his character as, someday, some discerning girl with the patience to chip away would find out.

He looked at her with mute eyes and she knew she had made a miserable mistake. In his brash way, Bob had sensed before she did that she was reaching out to him, but he obviously hadn't understood just what she was reaching out for.

At that moment, not knowing where David was, with the suspicion burning in her mind that he and Justine had slipped away together to steal some time alone, there would have been a cold satisfaction in unfaithfulness, but not with Bob. Not because she didn't have enough affection for him, but because she had too much. She would not destroy him, use his devotion to steal a fleeting moment of time with which to assuage her heartache over David.

For both their sakes, for the sake of a lasting and worthwhile friendship, she must guide them back from this dangerous edge. The adoration on his face must never be allowed to spill out into words. That old cliché, being cruel to be kind, slid into her mind.

She tossed her head back and let the brittleness of her smile shatter the tenderness of the moment and the fragility of his hopes. "In fact, Bob, if I weren't so crazy about that wretch of a husband of mine, I could fancy you myself."

He was not slow on the uptake; he got the message.

"Thanks, Trina, but I know my rating with women. I'm not going to waste time talking about someone as dull as me. Let's talk about you instead."

"I love David, I want to make that perfectly clear, but that doesn't mean that I'm blind to other men. You really are nice, Bob."

"Yeh. Perhaps I've been in David's shadow too long. It was one heck of a surprise when he shot off home and came back with a wife. I hadn't realized he was that seriously tied up with anyone. How long have you known him?"

"Forever. He was twelve when he first saw me. I was in my crib at the time."

"So he watched you grow up and waited his chance?"

She began to breathe easier; the danger had passed. It was going to be all right between them. "He couldn't stand me. When I was eighteen I had a terrible crush on him. He made it plain that he thought I was a pain in the neck."

"If that's true, and I don't believe it, he obviously changed his mind, wise man." Then Bob demonstrated what a truly generous man he was by saying, "He's a great guy and I'm glad that someone like you happened to him. He works too hard. This venture has been his wife, his mistress, his baby. He's lived with it, slept with it, breathed life into it for three years. It's so near to being fully operational that I suppose he finds it difficult to let up now."

Perhaps—and she hoped this was the case—it had been nothing more than a moment of madness and Bob was relieved that they were back on the old footing.

"That's in case I've been feeling neglected," she said, without having to exercise too much perception.

"I sometimes think, for all his knowledge of women, he doesn't know them at all."

"What do you mean, Bob, 'all his knowledge of women'?" she asked with exaggerated teasing.

He grimaced. "That's just the sort of fool remark I make when I'm trying to smooth things out. Who needs enemies when they've got friends like me? And why don't I just keep my big mouth shut?"

"It's all right," she said, relenting. "I know there have been others. At his age, I couldn't expect to be the first girl in his life."

"So long as you're the last, hey?"

"I suppose I can hope for that," she said, but without conviction. Opting to get off that aspect of David's life, she regarded Bob thoughtfully. "David's not the only one to have worked hard or given up three years. You have too."

"And never regretted a day of it. It's been the most rewarding job I've ever tackled. And I don't just mean the pay, although that's not a consideration to be sniffed at. It's like this—when you think of the term 'financier' it conjures up a picture of a man sitting behind a huge desk puffing on a big fat cigar, pushing buttons, and expecting miracles. It's great being in with someone who's there not just to crack the whip now and then, but has a working involvement. Someone who sees at first hand all the problems that need to be dealt with and isn't afraid of rolling up his sleeves when it's required."

That surprised her. She hadn't realized that Geoffrey Hyland, the financier Bob was obviously referring to, was part of the working team. She'd thought that he probably descended on them, from time to time, to keep an eye on his investment, leaving David in charge of the actual carrying out of the work. She seemed to have misjudged the man, in one way at least.

It was on the tip of her tongue to say what she thought, but Bob forestalled her. "See what I mean? Only an oaf like me would talk shop in the company of a pretty girl. Would you like to dance?"

"I'd love to," she replied promptly.

As they made their way to join the dancers, she said, "Have you seen Ginny this evening?"

"No."

"I'd make a point of it, if I were you. She looks quite something."

"That'll be the day. Poor kid, she's got no fashion sense, and that awful brown ribbon she wears in her hair . . ." His eyes closed in despair. "I ask you!"

"Her hair isn't tied back tonight. She's wearing green."

"I'll bet she looks just like a string bean."

"If I took that bet on I could have your boot laces," she said.

"Okay, so she looks more presentable than usual. I'm just not that curious to find out. I see enough of her during the day with—" His eyes narrowed on Petrina's huge smile. "So, what's the joke?"

"Nothing much. Just something that crossed my mind." When indifference was laid on this thickly, didn't it sometimes mean the opposite? Was Bob more impressed with Ginny than he made out?

With no more warning than a flicker of lightning across the sky, the rain began to fall. Or perhaps she had used all her senses to sort things out with Bob and she hadn't been alerted to the fact that the storm was ready to break.

Someone had, she thought, on realizing that the long tables and benches and most of the implements of the barbecue had been carried away and that the crowd had thinned considerably. Only the musicians remained and a handful of dancers who wanted to squeeze the last drop of enjoyment out of the evening.

"Where's David? Have you seen him anywhere?"

"No, and I'm not staying around to look," Bob said.

At least, that's what she thought he'd said. The tail end of his words was lost in a gigantic roar of thunder. The sky opened and it poured down. It was totally unlike England's gentle rain. It bent her to its will, driving and battering and soaking her within seconds. It felt as though she were walking in a river. Bob's arm had immediately clamped around her and within its protection she was raced back to the hotel. Sliding and slipping, she was grateful of that arm around her shoulders, then under her legs, as he became hampered by and impatient of her slowness and lifted her up and ran, carrying her for the rest of the way.

He dumped her on the hotel steps, his eyes urgently scanning the giggling, bedraggled group of people huddled there. Petrina, too, searched for a face that wasn't there.

"I wonder where David's got to," she said.

Bob said wryly, "If I were you I'd go straight upstairs and get out of those wet clothes."

"Good idea." She turned obediently in the direction of the elevator, but hesitated when she realized it wasn't Bob's intention to follow her. "Where are you going?"

"I just thought I'd take a look outside."

"What for? If David hasn't the sense to come in out of the rain then he deserves to get wet," she said tartly. "Anyway, he's probably sheltering somewhere."

"Mm, yes."

He was wearing a silly, self-conscious grin on his

face. Ginny's also seemed to be a missing face among the crowd. Of course! It wasn't David he was concerned about at all.

David followed her up practically on her heels, before she'd had time to change out of her sodden clothes. She was in a sorry, bedraggled state; his appearance hadn't altered.

"You're not even wet," she accused.

"I was in the car. There was something I remembered that had to be done. I expected to be back before the storm broke, but no doubt Bob looked after you."

How dare he have the effrontery to throw Bob in her face! She'd seen him dancing with Justine just before they both disappeared. She didn't need to have it spelled out just what the nature of the mission was that had taken him off with such urgency.

She threw back her head. "Yes, he did," she said, adding with taunting deliberation, "Bob is a perfect gentleman."

"Meaning I'm not?"

She shrugged. "If you say so."

He grasped her angrily by the shoulders. "I suppose *he* wouldn't have left you kicking your heels these last two days?"

Had she only been here two days? Was it only three days since their wedding? It seemed a lifetime ago since she'd kissed her father-in-law, dear Uncle Richard, goodbye and embarked on her new life with such love for her husband, such high optimism. The love was still there—no matter how difficult he was or how despicably he behaved, she would always love him—but her optimism was fast diminishing. She was too spirited to turn a blind eye to his affair with another woman and take a place in the background, grateful for the little affection he could spare. It seemed incredible that he would expect it of her after only three days of marriage.

"You've got to bear in mind that Bob doesn't have my responsibilities," he said through clenched teeth.

What was all this talk about Bob, if not to divert her from asking questions about Justine?

"What responsibilities?" she demanded recklessly. "Do you mean he doesn't have a mistress to pacify?"

"I must presume you mean Justine?" he queried with heavy sarcasm.

"You presume correctly."

"Jealous, Pet?" he mocked.

His cool derision was more difficult to bear than his earlier anger. She had nothing handy to throw at him except words. She had plenty of those.

"Of course not! You've got to care something for a person before you can be jealous. Remember, I only married you because it was preferable to remaining at home and being harassed by the press." Her heart sorrowed at the lie, but her pride rejoiced in it.

"Ah, yes." He tilted her chin and forced her to meet his glance head-on. "And have you worked out yet why I married you—apart from lusting for you, that is?"

She ran her tongue nervously over her dry lips. She was wishing she hadn't been drawn into this—at the same time she refused to back down. "Yes, I worked that out practically straight away."

"Tell me what you worked out." When she didn't reply, he commanded, "Answer me."

"Do you need enlightening?" She would not *let* him frighten her, or, more to the truth, she would not let him know that he *was* frightening her.

"No. I know my reason for marrying you." His

mouth twisted on cruel self-indulgence. "I thought it might be amusing to hear your theory."

"I can't see any reason for not telling you. You married me to throw your boss off the scent. Whatever his suspicions before, he would hardly think you were still carrying on with his wife when you turned up with a bride."

He smiled as though he really was amused by her reasoning. She must remember that he was clever. Beneath the smile she could sense that he was seething, so he was probably aiming to ridicule her to make her think she was wrong.

"My boss?" he queried.

"Who else but Geoffrey Hyland," she said in a voice equally as imperious as his. "He *is* your boss, isn't he?"

"No." Hauteur overlaid his tone. "He's my partner. We are both shareholders."

"I guessed as much. I'd an idea you'd invested money of your own and that you weren't just an employee. But isn't there one person who makes the decisions, pushes the buttons, and can take full blame for creating, out of my father's loss, a holiday island that combines everything he most detested? In other words, isn't there a major shareholder?"

"Yes, there is," he said, his eyes narrowing to points of steel.

Didn't he know she understood that he was carrying out someone else's orders and that her criticism wasn't directed at him?

It seemed not. He replied as though it was a personal attack on his integrity and the words exploded from him. "All the arguments lead back to this one point, don't they, Petrina? You're blinded by false loyalty. You can't see that your father's dream was just that.

121

Dreams are mental fantasies. They're not meant to convert to reality. Your father found that out and it destroyed him. Anybody foolish enough to pour his money into a vision that's impractical and doesn't have a sound base to build on would be destroyed too." He pulled himself up. Concern for her locked with his anger and overtook it. "I know I'm being unkind. It's too soon after your father's death for all this. I'm not so insensitive that I don't know you're grieving for him."

She would not be placated. "Y–you're n–not acting in an insensitive or unkind way. You're merely being true to form." Only her voice faltered. Her intention to hurt him, as he had hurt her, was steadfast.

"Dear heaven, it's hopeless!" It was a cry of anguish. "Why won't you see, damn you? Gingerbread houses crumble underfoot. Sugar-icing castles melt in the rain. Prince Divinely Perfect doesn't exist. Come down to earth and accept what you've got—an ordinary guy with ordinary desires and ordinary faults. Accept me, Petrina, just as I am. If you don't, one day you'll look around and you won't have me any longer, because I'm getting mighty fed up of being looked down on as though I were trash."

"Now who's being unfair? I've never looked down on you and you know it."

A feeling of uneasy guilt touched her heart. She didn't pause to analyze it, but acted on it with childish impulsiveness—at least that's what she wanted to believe. She didn't think it was sexual desire that prompted her to slide her arms up around his neck. Even though, in the passion of anger, he had never looked more attractive, it was a gesture of comfort and not an act of seduction.

She couldn't believe it when he cruelly twisted her

linked fingers apart and thrust her away. His eyes flicked over her face with cold contempt. "No, Petrina, not that way. I've no time for a woman who offers her body to end an argument."

Hot color rushed into her cheeks, but no ready reply sprang to her lips. She would never have thought that he held her in such low esteem that he could think that of her. It shocked her and it angered her and the curl of warm feeling inside her rolled into a ball of ice.

"I may as well tell you now as later," he said in a tone as stinging as a whiplash. "Geoff Hyland is due to arrive first thing tomorrow morning."

"Oh?" She was fighting for the control he could achieve at will.

"I shall be tied up with him for the biggest part of the day. In effect, it will be a winding-up operation, making it possible for me to take a couple of weeks off. I couldn't think of taking a break until certain matters had been settled with him. I got in touch with him by phone on the day we were married, but because of other commitments, tomorrow's the earliest time he could make it. He said he would like to meet you. It would be discourteous of me to refuse, so I've arranged for the four of us to have dinner together tomorrow evening."

"The four of us?" she gasped, and the thimbleful of control she had managed to scoop up drained away, taking her color with it.

"As Geoff's wife, naturally Justine will be there." His raised eyebrow reverted to its normal position as he said, "Then we'll be able to slip away on our honeymoon."

Away from the false atmosphere of the hotel, away from the demands of the job, away from people. It was what she had most wanted. But what a mockery it would be to share a dinner table with her husband's mistress before going away on her honeymoon. Sitting at the same table as Justine at the barbecue had been an ordeal, but this was worse! David had arranged this. How could he humiliate her in this way?

Chapter Eight

So that's why Justine and David had slipped away from the barbecue. They had grasped what might be their last opportunity of being alone together before Justine's husband arrived and David made the token gesture of taking his bride on a honeymoon. Afterward, when Geoffrey Hyland's suspicions were lulled, they would be free to meet at their discretion.

She had no idea what she was going to do about this. As yet her mind wouldn't form a plan, but she couldn't see herself cooperating blindly without putting up a fight.

When this bogus honeymoon was over, David would return to Chimera to take up his duties. Would she come back with him? Her tormented brain could supply no answer.

She lay in bed with her lashes closed so he wouldn't see her wounded eyes. Her body was stiff in rejection.

To no account, however, because he made no approach to share her bed—neither did he offer to touch her. Perverse creature that she was, this didn't suit her either.

The atmosphere at breakfast the next morning was normal in that David was preoccupied with the things he had to get through during the day. She wondered where he was taking her for their honeymoon, a curiosity she indulged by asking him.

"That's my surprise," he said mysteriously.

"What about the packing? Shall I do yours as well as my own?"

He didn't question her docility. Always alert to her mood, he probably knew it was a deceptive meekness, a thin crust covering volcanic thoughts. "Just see to your own," he instructed, adding as an afterthought, making her wonder if he'd read her mind to the extent of knowing she was considering the possibility of not coming back with him, "You only need to take sufficient to tide you over for two weeks. The rest of your things will be safe left here. This suite is permanently reserved for me."

"I'd gathered as much," she said stiffly. "What kind of clothes do I take? I don't want to spoil your secret, but it would be as well to know what kind of climate I'm packing for."

"Much the same as this," he said, a taut smile coming to his mouth as though she'd said something amusing.

"Will I see you at lunchtime?"

"That's highly improbable. I'll most likely grab a working lunch."

"In that case, have you any objection to my getting a packed lunch and spending the day on the beach?"

"Not at all. I think it's an excellent idea." A twinkle came to his eye, dark, mischievous. "Be sure to wear your sun hat. I don't want you getting sunstroke again, my love."

"You are so solicitous," she said, giving him a false smile.

He dropped a kiss on her cheek. "Bye for now, Pet."

Wearing her swimsuit under her sun dress, just in case, and armed with her packed lunch, her sun hat firmly positioned on her head, she left the hotel complex and walked in the direction of the beach. Her skin was more acclimatized now and would have stood an hour or two's sunning, but it was not her plan to sunbathe. She intended to follow the goat's body shape of the coastline and curve around to where the serpent's tail flicked sharply away from view. She knew she could not leave Chimera—possibly for good, because she still hadn't made up her mind whether she was staying with David or opting for her freedom— without first investigating this intriguing hidden place.

It was hot walking. After a while she took her sandals off and padded along the water's edge, reveling in the cool tingle as the waves lapped her feet and splashed her legs. Anticipation urged her on. She was optimistically certain that something wonderful was waiting to be discovered. She knew she could have found a shorter and more direct route by road, but this way, following the curve of the coastline, she entered more into the spirit of the thing.

Eventually she did have to leave the beach and take the road before she could reach the point where she would know if it had been worthwhile or if it was a case of having yet another illusion shattered.

And then, suddenly, it was all laid out before her feet, and it was even more beautiful than she had thought it would be. She stood staring at it, her eyes filled with exquisite wonder. It was the little bay, the one depicted on the postcard she'd sent to Uncle Richard that had so captured her heart. This was the real Chimera, the realization of her father's dream.

Turquoise sea lapping white sand. Peace and isolation. There was an addition to the bay that hadn't been on the postcard: a house that had obviously been built since it was taken. It was long and low, comprising two stories, with grilled ironwork balconies marking the upper floor and shutters at every window. Creamy white oleander, purple bougainvillaea, and a vine of spiky petalled blood-red flowers trailed their beauty down the white-painted pillars and walls and flowed over the slatted woodwork of the wide veranda. In a natural setting of palm trees, in perfect taste with this paradisiacal setting, it far exceeded anything her imagination could have dreamed up. It was—oh, how inadequate her mind was, drugged by such eye-enchanting, joy-to-behold beauty—just *perfect*.

She longed to venture down the winding path, steal a closer look at the house, sit on the white sand, and stare dreamily out to sea, but she thought she might be trespassing on a private beach.

Even as she was trapped in thought, wondering hesitantly if she dare go closer, a woman came lumbering up the path. A typically round-hipped *señora*, all in black. She came from the direction of the house and, judging by her clothes, was probably the cleaning woman.

Her smile was wide and friendly as she called out, "*Buenos días.*"

"*Buenos días, señora,*" Petrina responded. "I was just admiring the house," she said in English.

"*Qué?*" the *señora* muttered, obviously not understanding her.

128

Petrina searched her brain. What was Spanish for pretty? *"Muy bonita."*

Ah, *sí."* The woman nodded her head and pointed to Petrina. *"Inglesa?"*

"Yes, I'm English. Can you speak any English?"

"A little," the *señora* said carefully, pronouncing it "leetle."

"Is this a private beach?"

"Qué?"

She tried again. "Who owns this? Who does the *casa* belong to?"

The *señora* looked puzzled for a moment and then her smile beamed in understanding. *"El señor jefe.* Good man. Bring work and—how do you say it?— richness to Chimera. *Tengo siete niños."* She clicked her tongue. "I forget. I speak English. I have children." She held up seven fingers. "You understand?"

Petrina nodded to say she did. The *señora* was telling her she had seven children.

"They all go away. No jobs on Chimera. Now is different. They all come back. My sons, they have work on roads. My daughters in hotels." She patted her pockets. "Plenty money. *El señor jefe,* good man." With a friendly wave of her hand she departed.

"Adiós, señora," Petrina called after her.

Even before the woman had gone into detail, Petrina had recognized the word *jefe.* It meant top man, the chief. So this delightful house and, presumably, this secluded bay belonged to Geoffrey Hyland.

She knew she would now regard him in an entirely different and much more favorable light. Her opinion of him underwent a total change. Because of what he'd done to Chimera she'd thought he was a ruthless business tycoon with no finer feelings, but she had the evidence of her own eyes that this was not so—he was not insensitive to beauty. He'd made the project pay by giving tourists what they wanted. He'd brought content and prosperity to the people of Chimera and, if everyone was of the same mind as the *señora,* earned their everlasting adoration. At the same time, he'd kept faith with his own ideals by preserving for his own use this small corner of the island in the image of her father's dream.

Now that she had a revised picture of him in her mind, she didn't think Geoffrey Hyland would object to her trespassing on his property, so she made her way down to his house. Once there, she couldn't see in because of the shutters, but she walked all the way around it and approved of everything she saw: the typically Spanish wrought-iron outside staircase; the tubs of exotic flowers that had remarkably escaped too severe a battering from last night's storm; the statuary in stone and marble. In particular, she lost her heart to a half-naked nymph whose marble mouth lifted in a sweet Madonna smile. The windows behind the semi-circular balconies were positioned to welcome the morning sun. But in the heat of midday it was the shady promise of the veranda that was most tempting. It would have been pleasant to walk along the cool tiles, cooled by the gentle breeze, and let the utter loveliness of it all soak right through her soul.

Had Geoffrey Hyland been in residence, she felt certain he would have bestowed this privilege upon her, but he wasn't, and she was inhibited by protocol. It wasn't the thing to do to take his consent for granted to this extent, so she sat on the white sand—it didn't seem as much like trespass—and unpacked her picnic lunch. Coming upon the house like this had been a very moving and beautiful experience, bringing memories of her father that were almost too strong to bear. She sat with her eyes facing out to sea while she ate, but she couldn't see a thing for the tears.

She arrived back at the hotel with plenty of time to pack and get ready for dinner. She was now keenly looking forward to meeting Geoffrey Hyland, anticipating the event with joy that was only slightly moderated by the daunting prospect of also sharing a table with Justine.

She chose an evening dress in the same turquoise shade as the sea in the serpent's tail bay. Serpent's tail might describe the shape of the coastline, but it wasn't a very apt name. No part of a serpent belonged in that sweet corner of paradise.

She rarely used much makeup and now, with the bloom of the sun on her skin, barely needed any at all beyond a finger smear of eye shadow on her lids and a gentle application of lip gloss. She brushed her hair to bring out the copper and gold highlights, coaxing and smoothing it with her fingers to achieve the desired effect. Finally she sprayed her pulse spots with her favorite perfume, which was light, flowery, and non-cloying. If confidence in one's appearance guaranteed poise, she should be all right.

David appeared at the last possible moment, packed in minutes, showered, and dressed with one eye on the clock.

She saw that he was wearing the gray suit he'd been married in.

"I didn't think you were going to make it," she said with a lump in her throat.

"Nor I."

He looked worn out. She hoped he'd picked a quiet spot for their honeymoon—somewhere that would allow him to empty his mind and relax completely. Physically, he was in outwardly excellent shape, but mentally and emotionally, at least, he badly needed a rest. She didn't know if the lump had come to her throat because he'd chosen to wear that suit, or because she wanted to put her fingers up to his face and smooth away the lines of fatigue and strain.

"I've got a present for you," he said, carelessly handing her a package.

When unwrapped it revealed an exquisitely worked shawl. It was so light it was almost weightless, and more beautiful than any of those she had seen and coveted in the local shops, although it was obviously the work of a Chimeran woman.

"Thank you," she said, her smile glowing in appreciation. "It's beautiful."

Draping it around her shoulders, he said, "So are you. You look very lovely. So very young. Geoff will accuse me of cradle snatching." She had an idea he was going to add something to that. Words of support, comfort, or even advance information about the man she was going to meet. The impression of something formed in his eyes, but all he said was, "We're meeting up in the bar for a drink. Are you ready?"

She picked up her evening bag and nodded solemnly.

As they walked into the bar, a comprehensive look around located their dinner companions. Justine was all in black again, save for her scarlet lips and fingernails. Her shoulders gleamed palely through the black lace of the bodice, leaf motifed for modesty. It hugged her figure, accentuating her beautiful body. Although more daring than anything Petrina would have cared to wear, it was without doubt the most feminine, most elegant, prettiest dress she had ever seen. It suited Justine to perfection.

Her eyes hurried on to the man by Justine's side. He was older than she had expected, with a thin, intelligent face and silvery hair. He was not much, if at all, taller than Justine.

In guiding her forward to where the others stood, David's hand closed possessively around her elbow. It was very much an act of ownership. Nothing on his face suggested that he could possibly guess at the thoughts surging through her head; only the gentle squeeze of his fingers told of this insight and gave sympathetic support.

"The ladies, I believe, have met. Darling, may I present my friend and colleague, Geoffrey Hyland. Geoff, my wife, Petrina."

"How do you do?" Geoffrey Hyland said very correctly, taking her hand in a handshake that was so light it had no substance behind it, but making up for this in the quality of the look he gave her.

His eyes were a dark, penetrating gray-black and seemed to search out all the pockets of her brain. His expensively tailored lightweight suit was worn, as were a ring set with a huge diamond and a wafer-thin watch, with the easy elegance of someone who is used to wealth. His slight build only lightly masked the air of power and authority that exuded from him. The deception of the gentle handshake tricked her for only a matter of seconds. She knew she was in the presence of a cold, calculating, and utterly ruthless man, a despot who would use his power without conscience and be pitiless in his dealings with others.

Realizing that David had asked her twice what she would like to drink, she came out of her stupefaction and said the first thing that came into her head. "An iced lemon drink, please."

It was pure luck that it was a choice that coincided with her desperate need to quench her parched throat. She was shattered by her first-hand assessment of Geoffrey Hyland. Surely she must be wrong?

The talk as they sipped their predinner drinks was the usual inconsequential social banter. She tried to relax, but she was too deeply conscious of Geoffrey Hyland's eyes upon her to do so with any measure of success. The harder she strove for tranquillity, the more impossible it was to achieve. She couldn't help shivering under the surveillance of that cold, stripping look. When he complimented her on her appearance, remarking how charming he thought her dress was, she managed to bring out a responsive smile, knowing full well that it was the merchandise beneath and not the wrapping that engaged his interest.

With implicit meaning, Justine said, "I was thinking myself how well that color suits you. You should wear it more often. It really is most flattering." All this as if Petrina didn't usually look as good and the effect had been acquired by accident.

"I'll make a note of it," she replied coolly, and bit her lip on the smarting retort that she would have liked to make.

She was enough in the wrong with David as it was. It was such a usual occurrence that she didn't have to labor to read what was behind the frown on his face. She knew that he thought she was being deliberately difficult and unsociable.

He smoothed out his features to repay Geoffrey Hyland's compliment to her by telling Justine how lovely she looked. *Ravishing* was the actual word he used.

A twisted little smile played on Geoffrey Hyland's

thin lips. It said more clearly than words could that he knew of the liaison between his wife and David. It was no coincidence, she thought, that throughout the meal Geoffrey Hyland chose to be particularly attentive to her.

The ceremony of the meal, which was more like a banquet with its many exotic courses, was as much of an ordeal to Petrina as the company, even though the waiter was in league with her. Perhaps it was part of his training to observe such things but, on noticing her dilemma when faced with a full plate, with thoughtful discretion he began to serve her with smaller portions.

"The chef has excelled himself tonight. That lobster was truly delicious," Geoffrey Hyland said, patting his lips with his napkin.

It had been served in a spicy sauce, and now that her portions were more manageable, Petrina's empty plate was in total agreement.

She knew that by drawing her out, by talking to her, Geoffrey Hyland was endeavoring to be kind, but his manner was overfond, cloying, like that of a womanizer. She tried to like him. She remembered the house in the unspoiled serpent's tail bay. Its creator must be a man of discriminating taste and deep sensitivity. But search as she might, she couldn't find any such streak in this autocratic man whose smile seemed to point at a perverse sense of humor. This was borne out by the fact that he gave no indication of minding that Justine was flirting outrageously with David. He seemed to find it all highly amusing, in fact—a performance put on especially for his entertainment.

One thing emerged clearly. There was no plot—or if there was, Justine wasn't in on it—to introduce a new wife to the scene to put a suspicious husband off the scent. Justine didn't care. She was quite blatant in her attitude toward David, charming and cajoling him and pouting her lip at him when he continued to remain grim-mouthed and unresponsive to her coquetry.

Petrina put her dessert spoon down on the remains of an epicurean's delight of cream and cake and fresh fruit, aware that coffee would be served in their choice of the several lounges. A quiet lounge with deep armchairs to relax in. A television lounge. A lounge where tables were set up for after-dinner card games. Or a lounge with a space cleared in the center for those energetic enough to want to dance.

On leaving the dining room, Justine made the decision and led the way to the lounge that gave out strains of music. Already the lively beat of a group had tempted one or two couples onto the floor.

"Geoff will order the coffee, won't you, darling? David, dance with me." Justine's slender hand strayed possessively to David's shoulder, denying him the right to refuse.

He sent Petrina a slight shrug, as if to say he wasn't interested in her opinion, and took Justine onto the dance floor.

Geoffrey Hyland said, "You must not mind my wife, Petrina—I may be permitted to call you by your first name, I trust?" She nodded to give her permission and he continued. "She is like a naughty child who can't bear to have her nose put out of joint. She has always flirted with David and he has been too kind to rebuff her. Perhaps he has been . . . 'kinder' . . . than we shall ever know. He is having to suffer for his gallantry now and finding it quite a strain. Don't you think so?"

"I don't know what to think, Mr. Hyland."

"Come, please, you must call me Geoffrey." He pressed his hand over hers, and although his touch sent a shudder through her body, she tried to conceal her revulsion by not dragging her fingers away.

"Thank you, Geoffrey," she said, tentatively testing his name on her lips. "I'm baffled by your frankness. Wouldn't it be better to pretend not to know about them instead of so obviously condoning their behavior?"

"For David's sake, perhaps it would. It must be distressing for him to have his indiscretions played out before the eyes of his lovely bride, but no one gets away scot-free in this life. David should have known that eventually he would have to pay for his fun."

She now hated Geoffrey Hyland intensely. What she had taken to be a slightly mischievous, if dubious, sense of humor was evil. She wished David would come back and rescue her from his wicked, cruel tongue. But David was still dancing with Justine, and the music showed no signs of letting up. She was trapped.

"As for my wife," Geoffrey Hyland continued smoothly, tormentingly, "can't you see how much she's enjoying extracting payment?"

"Doesn't it bother you?"

"No. I like to see her enjoying herself."

"Don't you mind that she's—"

"Unfaithful to me? That's the proper term, Petrina, so you shouldn't be afraid to use it. A too faithful wife can be a shackle. I, too, like to feel free of restrictions. You have very expressive eyes, my dear. I can tell you are shocked. Don't be. It's perfectly normal for couples who have been married a number of years to go their separate ways. As you will find out."

She shook her head in growing perplexity. "No, never! Wouldn't divorce be a more honorable solution?"

"You are charmingly naive. The settlement a wife

can claim makes it too costly. As extravagant as Justine is, it's cheaper to keep her as a wife than to divorce her."

"But you're a very wealthy man. You don't have to concern yourself about the cost of anything."

"I concern myself because I intend to keep my wealth, not dissipate it in that way. Divorce is habit forming. If you do it once, it's easier the next time. I could find myself going through the whole costly business several times over. So you see, it's better this way."

"No, I don't see. And I never will," she said with passionate resistance.

"I'm sorry, my dear. I did not mean to upset you. Now I feel dreadful. Especially as it was my intention to apologize to you for delaying the start of your honeymoon. I got here as soon as I could. As you probably know, David needed to discuss certain matters of finance with me before feeling free to depart. Can you forgive me?"

"Of course. There's nothing to forgive."

"As sweet as you are forgiving. What a charming nature you have. And what a fool David is. I would never be so dedicated to duty that I would delay my honeymoon, especially if my bride were as lovely as you. You have an enchanting innocence that I have never known in a woman. Perhaps if I'd met someone like you when I was younger, I wouldn't be such a wicked old cynic now. I even venture to say that if I met someone like you now, I might be prepared to change my views on divorce. But this is not the time to go too deeply into the matter. In a year or two, when the novelty of your marriage has worn off, we might reopen this conversation, yes?"

"No, I think not," she said, aware that her blush was

rising under the keen penetration of his eyes, trying with extreme difficulty not to show her dislike too much because it wasn't a polite thing to do. Which was a laugh, really, on her upbringing if nothing else, because Geoffrey Hyland was not observing the social code of niceties, so why should she?

To her great relief, Justine and David returned.

Justine said, "That was fantastic. Where's the coffee, darling?"

That sardonic smile came to Geoffrey Hyland's lips. "Sorry, my angel; Petrina and I were so engrossed in our conversation that I didn't get around to ordering it."

"Not to worry," Justine said amiably, "no hurry. I hope they play a rumba for us next, David."

Petrina was wondering how David was going to extricate himself, or even if he wanted to, when Geoffrey Hyland effected the release for him.

Smiling, he said, "I obeyed a selfish impulse in asking to meet Petrina, but we must remember that it is the child's honeymoon. You must not monopolize the bridegroom."

Petrina suspected that Geoffrey Hyland had not spoken out of consideration for her, but merely to thwart his wife, who shrugged her shoulders and showed her displeasure in a sulky look.

Geoffrey Hyland snapped his fingers to alert a waiter, but before he had time to order the coffee, David said, "Make it for two. It's time we were on our way."

Justine's eyes narrowed on Petrina in acute antipathy, but she said nothing. Not even goodbye.

David's hand came out as though to go around Petrina's waist, but she skipped ahead of him, her jaw rigid. She had to fight to stop herself from breaking into a run, so desperate was the urge to get away from Justine and her horrible husband as quickly as possible. Her mind was in equal turmoil. She had such a lot of things to puzzle over, but no time to do so now. Why had David married her? It was not, as she had thought, to blind Justine's husband to the truth. So why? How could such a vile man as Geoffrey Hyland have the good taste to build that elegant house in that beautiful, unadulterated setting? And then her thoughts swung back again. *Why had David married her?* Geoffrey Hyland *encouraged* his wife to have affairs, because it gave him the freedom to do the same, so . . .

Her wrist was taken in the steel clamp of David's fingers. "Don't struggle, darling, you'll only cause a scene. Simmer down; you're smoldering."

She swallowed on anger that shrouded her like a mist. "That vile man. His *eyes.* The way he looked at me. I felt—" His eyes had ravished her in full public view. She felt unclean and had some inkling of how a rape victim must feel. She modified her thoughts and said—"insulted."

His reading of what she'd deliberately not said could account for the violence of his frown. Yet, puzzlingly, she felt part of the condemnation was vented against her. "He wouldn't consider it an insult to find you desirable in that way. I've seen that look in another man's eyes and you haven't cringed away from him."

She faltered at the scathing accusation. "You're referring to yourself, of course?"

"Actually, I wasn't," he retorted, regarding her thoughtfully and rewarding her perplexity with a milder tone. "I'm sorry that it was necessary to inflict tonight on you. Business colleagues are rarely chosen on a personal basis. My opinion of Geoff Hyland is much the same as yours, but I have to put up with him."

Why? her brain shouted furiously. To be near Justine? "Well, I don't," she said angrily.

She should have known that he would not let that go unchallenged. He stopped walking. Much as she longed to stride on ahead, his hand on her wrist prevented it.

"I'm sorry to correct you, Pet," he said in an insidiously quiet voice, "but you'll have to put up with it if I say so. You're my wife. You have to accept the people I'm involved with."

Did he mean Justine? She was choking on hurt and temper. "Would you accept it if it were the other way around?"

He replied disparagingly, "Speculation has got to have a sound footing. The question of whether I could accept your doubtful acquaintances is unlikely to arise."

"What do you mean by that?" she asked, immediately on the defensive.

"Don't be so prickly. I merely meant that it would be inconceivable to find such a character in your little world."

She was not appeased. On the contrary, his satirical tone heightened her suspicions. "Are you sniping at my father? I know he wasn't always respectable in his business dealings."

"I was not. Your father was more foolish than dishonest. I didn't think you had a complex about that."

"I haven't. It's just—" Her slender shoulders lifted in a gesture that spelled out the futility of trying to explain what she didn't properly understand herself.

She didn't know how lost or desolate she looked, so she didn't know why his face settled into such grim lines or the reason for the tone of his voice. It was so tense it seemed in danger of snapping off midsentence. "Let's get out of here. I left instructions for our cases to be brought down and put in the car. Have you anything to go up for?"

"I'd like to change, please, if there's time. Is there? I don't fancy boarding a plane dressed like this."

"You have time to do anything you may desire," he said with scantily veiled implication. "But did I say anything about boarding a plane?"

"No, you didn't."

Ruling out the slight possibility that they were going somewhere by boat, because she was just as unsuitably dressed for that, it meant their honeymoon destination was somewhere on the island. Curiosity was a minor thing and barely registered in her thoughts. It was unimportant where they went.

A quiver of passionate urgency leaped between them. Every pulse in her body was beating out her awareness of him. Her nerve ends were jumping, stimulated to respond by the torrid dominance of his eyes.

Drawing a ragged breath, she said, "I've still got to go up. I want to take my other handbag with me."

His mouth closed on a small teasing smile that was, curiously, mocking and tender at the same time, and he seemed to make a tentative exploration into thought. "I suppose I could fetch it for you."

"Thank you. That's considerate of you."

"Perhaps you should come with me. It may be more considerate of me than you think." His hand slid under her chin. "If I got you up to the privacy of our suite, we wouldn't be venturing out again too soon."

Wasn't he aware that she knew that? Just as she knew he wanted her to go up with him. That was what *she* wanted, too. She wasn't happy to be in constant discord with him; it was much more pleasant to tangle with him in passion. Her body was submissive to this thought—it had dismissed all differences and was ready to yield. Not so her mind. It was still too full of the recent encounter with Justine and her husband. Her body had forgiven, but her mind was still angry with David for causing her the humiliation of making her accept his mistress and that vile man. He'd been brutal in his insistence. She was his wife. She must do as she was told, and he had told her to accept the situation. She'd jumped to his inclination then; she would not be a puppet to his pleasure now.

"I'll keep you to your offer to fetch it for me." She tried to keep it cool, but was partially defeated by the bright patches of color in her cheeks. She could not include Justine and Geoffrey Hyland in her thoughts and keep all traces of revulsion from her expression.

"I see." His eyes turned to blue ice again, fixing on her with compelling, hypnotic brilliance.

"While you're gone, I'll try to find Ginny and Bob. I want to say goodbye to them."

"I'll go along with that, but watch it," he cautioned darkly.

"What do you mean?"

"Don't be obtuse. Bob's taken a tumble for you. He's not as hardy as I am, so don't try to wrap him around your finger."

Was he inferring that she'd *tried* to wrap him around her finger? The idea was so preposterous that she couldn't summon up the words to refute his statement about Bob.

"You can't deny that he's carrying a torch for you, can you?" he demanded abruptly.

Was it possible? Could he be jealous? She didn't know which surprised her the most—the fact that David might be jealous of the friendship and affection she and Bob shared or the reply that came startlingly to her lips. "I deny it most emphatically. The truth is, even if Bob has been slow to realize it, he's really crazy about Ginny."

The cold contempt in his laugh flicked over her. "Don't be ridiculous! They fight all the time."

"People in love do," she said quietly.

"Really?" he drawled. "By that piece of absurd reasoning, we must be very much in love."

He walked away, leaving her clenching her fingers on that bitter taunt.

Chapter Nine

Going through to the bar in search of Ginny and Bob, she was wryly amused to find them occupying adjacent bar stools. They weren't fighting now. Bob's arm was slung carelessly around Ginny's shoulders and Ginny's lively features had acquired a fascinating glow.

"Hello, Trina," Bob greeted on spotting her. "Honestly, I meant to come and see you off, but"—he grinned sheepishly—"I got waylaid."

"Don't believe him. I mean, who'd want to lay a trap for this big oaf?" Ginny chipped in predictably, while the smile on her face proudly proclaimed that the situation was firmly in hand.

"I'm glad, Ginny," Petrina said simply.

"Thanks, *amiga*," Ginny said.

Goodbyes were exchanged, and then she went back to wait for David. He didn't keep her waiting long.

"Let's go," he said, taking her arm and making her

run to keep up with his long stride. "It's best to make a speedy exit. There's always an emergency waiting to happen. If I'm not around someone else will have to deal with it." He was not apologizing—merely showing his awareness that he was rushing her.

"You do too much," she said. It was a soft protest, overshadowed by the happy prospect of getting away without further delay.

His car had been brought around to the front of the hotel. He waved away the man standing in attendance and opened the passenger door himself so she could get in. His zest for work—his ambition—was something she knew all about. But the importance he'd achieved was something that was going to take some getting used to. He opened his own door and slid behind the wheel.

She kept her eyes fixed on the windshield, her thoughts still very much in chaos. Despite his big pretense of urgency, David made no attempt to start the car, and eventually the uneasy silence that followed made her look at him. His eyes were directed to the front, but his thoughts, in keeping with hers, were turned inward. There was something reproachful about the forbidding hardness of his profile that stirred up an unpleasant torment in her.

Without warning his head turned around. Pinned under his dark gaze, her sensations of uneasiness grew. His hand touched her cheek, and lit a fire there that even the harshness of his laugh couldn't totally quench. No sound on earth could sound as cynical as his dry, weary, sarcastic "Mm."

His eyes continued to hold her on the knife edge of pain and remorse, feelings she tried to shake off by telling herself she had nothing to feel penitent about. "We communicate well enough physically, don't we, Pet?" he said, rotating his finger in the hollow of her cheek in a gesture that was pure sensuality. "But on all other levels we might as well be on different planets."

"We don't talk—is that what you mean?" Her voice seemed as tight and uncomfortable as she felt.

"That's precisely what I mean."

"That's not my fault, David."

"I'm not suggesting it is," he growled, but his tone belied his words and laid heavy censure on her heart.

He slammed the car door shut, mercifully putting out the interior light. The key, which had been left in the ignition, received a more vicious twist than usual.

It was unfair of him to blame her. Wasn't she the injured party? She would never forgive him for putting her through tonight's ordeal. It had taken her to the depths of degradation to be commanded to dine with Geoffrey Hyland and his beautiful but venomous wife, who had made it abundantly clear that she had no intention of relinquishing her claim on David. Petrina's whole body shuddered with mortified outrage. She didn't know which had filled her with the most revulsion—Geoffrey Hyland's greasy attentions to her or the explicit invitation in Justine's eyes as she had repeatedly caught and held David's glance. She'd heard about wife swapping. She supposed that started casually enough in light cross-flirtation in public places, but inevitably reached its end in more intimate surroundings.

For her the evening had possessed the unreality of a nightmare, yet she had been alone in holding herself cold and aloof from the proceedings. They had enjoyed what they seemed to regard as innocent fun. Innocent? Geoffrey Hyland had propositioned her right under David's nose. That brought her sharply up against another painful reminder—the short but very much to the point conversation she'd had with David immediately after leaving the Hylands. She had told him she would not put up with it. The cold menace of his reply would live forever in her mind: "I'm sorry to correct you, Pet, but you'll have to put up with it if I say so. You're my wife. You have to accept the people I'm involved with."

That had been his attitude, one he obviously intended to maintain, when he forced her to make up the foursome. Geoffrey Hyland had desired it. David had fallen in with his wishes. In his own words it would be discourteous of him to refuse to arrange the meeting. Just how far was David prepared to go to keep Geoffrey Hyland satisfied?

Geoffrey Hyland had made it very plain what else he desired. Her fresh young appeal had given potency to his jaded inclinations. He had probably tried everything, and had grown blasé. She had read in his hotly gleaming eyes that he wanted to go back to the beginning and capture, through her, the sweetness he had never known. Would David give in to him in this? Would he command her obedience in this matter against her will? Would he arrange *this* for Geoffrey Hyland?

She was so entrenched in the hurt of her thoughts that it was a while before she took note of the direction in which they were traveling. Surely this was the way she had come this morning when she discovered the secluded house in the cove, the paradisiacal secret of the serpent's tail.

An intriguing possibility came into her mind. She sat well back in her seat, not daring to hope. It would be too wonderful . . . too incredible. Even when they approached the turning-off point she expected him to keep his speed and continue straight ahead. But no, he was slowing . . . turning down the road where she had encountered the Spanish cleaning woman, and to her delight the car bumped its way down into the serpent's tail bay.

This morning she had blinked at the astonishing solitude and beauty of the bay in the fierce golden grip of the sun. Under the moon's domination it looked even more serenely enchanting than it had then.

The moon that had seemingly ensnared the sea in a shimmering net of stars held her in a dreamy, captive trance as she tried to puzzle out why, out of all the spots on the map David could have chosen, he'd brought her here. She hadn't told him of her feelings about this place, the enchanted hold it had on her, the strange, inexplicable aura of intrigue it possessed for her and her compulsion to discover the secret hidden from casual view by the curious twist of the coastline, the flick of the serpent's tail.

If only she could believe that David had brought her here to please her, because he knew there was no place on earth she would rather spend her honeymoon. It would not totally lift her depression—the feeling of being used and the humiliation she had been made to endure were not that quickly erased—but it would have eased it considerably if she could have thought that.

It was more feasible to believe there was a more mundane reason for his choice. Geoffrey Hyland was content to stay at the hotel. It would benefit the house to be opened up, no matter how diligently the cleaning woman took care of it, so he had granted the honeymooners temporary tenancy.

Her mouth was having trouble in deciding whether it wanted to curve up or down. The car engine had been quiet for much of the time she had been doing battle with her thoughts. It suddenly came to her how keenly David was studying her expression.

He said abruptly, unnecessarily, "We've arrived." He got out of his side of the car and came around to assist her out. He shut the car door after her, but his hand stayed on her arm. She had the good sense not to pull away. In a struggle, he would always win, and she didn't mean entirely because of his greater strength. Sometimes it's the gentle touch that brings a woman down.

As he began to guide her toward the house, she remembered something. "You've forgotten to get our suitcases."

"The morning will do. They're perfectly safe where they are."

"But—there are things I need. My nightgown, for instance."

"What's so essential about that?" The brilliance of the moon highlighted his expression. She didn't need to hear the taunting inflection in his voice to know that he was baiting her.

The moon's luminosity was turned full on this evening, casting its strong beam over the whole bay; in contrast, the shadows around the house plunged them into dramatic darkness. It was a dubious blessing. Walking from the ashen brilliance into the clinging pitchy murk of total obscurity served to conceal her flushed indignation, but it also gave him cause to say, "I'll put my arms around you so you don't stumble. Or perhaps . . . I've got a better idea."

Without telling her what form it took, he put it into effect, and she felt herself being picked up and carried up the steps, heart to heart. The only reason it wasn't also cheek to cheek was because she held her head stiffly averted.

Just short of the door, he said, "Do you want to go in?"

If she assented to that, she knew what she would be saying yes to. At the same time she knew that he wasn't delaying the moment out of consideration for her hurt feelings—at least, the hurt feelings might be an important factor but his motive in considering them was a selfish one. He appreciated everything about her that Geoffrey Hyland had appreciated and had much the same goal in mind, but there was one crowning difference. She was his wife. She was his without the need to go through the preliminary stages, the sweet and potent coaxing, the subtle and tantalizing delights of seduction as he worked on her emotions until her longing for him matched the devouring fire of his own demands. He knew what the fulfullment could be and he was throwing away his rights to win her over as a lover. He had once told her that he never took an unwilling woman to bed, and a wife who merely surrendered to him in docile duty would be little removed from that category.

She too had known the exultation of her blood turning to fire and kisses that were as total a commitment as the act of possession itself. Her blood danced in crazed response just thinking about it—but she would not yield to his desire on her own. It would be forced surrender or nothing. He could not put her through the agony he had put her through this evening and expect passion as well. If necessary, as she feared it would be, she would keep reminding herself, repeating to herself over and over again, that it was the ultimate in sadism and cruelty to make her dine at the same table as his mistress and subject her to the gloating and esteem-stripping debauchery of Geoffrey Hyland's eyes.

She inquired haughtily, "What alternative to going into the house do you have in mind?"

His tone of voice said, "It's like that, is it?" The actual words he used were: "It's much too pretty a night to go indoors."

It was, but if the atmosphere between them had been right that wouldn't have bothered him. Unless—unless he meant they should sleep out here, like nature children, on the sand?

"Go on," she said, gritting her voice on new determination.

"Have you ever gone for a swim by moonlight?"

"No."

"Does the idea appeal to you?"

It appealed to her better than the other idea that she thought had been running through his mind.

Her eyes flicked back and down to the car. "My swimsuit is in my suitcase."

He laughed, just as she knew he would. "What's the matter with the one you were born in? Nothing," he added before she could reply, "if my memory serves me right."

"I'm not going to refresh it. I either get my swimsuit or I don't swim."

"Okay, just this once. So don't let it go to your head."

"What?"

"Calling the tune," he said, whistling perfectly in tune himself as he set her down on her feet before moving quietly back down the steps. He returned with the two suitcases and her vanity case. His suitcase, she noticed, was impossibly small and obviously contained the barest essentials. Setting the cases down, he took a key from his pocket and inserted it in the lock. The key slid smoothly home with none of the usual initial awkwardness of fitting a strange key into a strange lock. Geoffrey Hyland was obviously generous with her husband when it came to giving him access to his house. Again without looking, with the ease of familiarity, he reached his hand around the door and flicked on the light switch.

She made a move to enter the house before him, but his fingers clamped around her wrist, deterring her. "We must observe tradition," he said drily.

"Of course." She submitted herself to being lifted into his arms and carried over the threshold. All part of the softening-up process, she reminded herself.

This morning, on venturing here, it had been too tantalizing not to be able to peep into the house and appease her curiosity, and now she was actually in the house and too full of being in David's arms to get more than the briefest impression of her surroundings.

Still carrying her, he moved forward, flicking on light switches as his feet trod purposefully across the mosaic-tiled floor, predominantly colored in misty blue and white, of the entrance hall. Her skimming gaze revealed furniture gleaming like dark wine against the white walls, providing the perfect foil for fragrant red flowers in a tall black vase. He made for the bedroom without detour or hesitation.

He set her down and then went back for the suitcases while she surveyed the bed. A very large double bed—not the twin beds that seemed to be the preference in hot countries and that she had expected to see.

She opened her suitcase and found her swimsuit without causing much disorder. Out of the corner of her painfully averted eye she saw that he was stripping off his clothes. With a small inevitable sigh she knew she must do the same, somehow keeping up her reserve. Frosty intentions and undressing at shoulder-to-shoulder proximity were difficult to mesh. Assessing the situation, she thought, This is my husband, the most devastatingly attractive man I've ever met and I'm so much in love with him I'm not seeing straight. Suddenly all her problems seemed insurmountable.

In her inattentiveness, her fingers jammed the long back zip of her dress. "Would you mind, please?" she asked, turning her back on him and lifting her hair clear.

"My pleasure." His fingers brushed the nape of her neck as he found the small tag. The contact was deliberate and found the reaction it sought. Encouraged by the revealing and treacherous quiver that went through her body, his mouth dropped a kiss on the exact spot his fingers had stirred into warmth with their light but sensuous touch.

She moved away as though she'd been burnt. As she had. Their passion, flaring into active response, was a dancing, tantalizing flame that was painful for her to stand aloof from or to contact. It was so tempting to let its heat consume her, to be as one with her husband, so much more tempting than struggling to escape.

He made it easy for her by not pressing home his advantage and completed the task she'd set him with stoic detachment. "Slowpoke," he said in gentle reprimand. "Join me when you're ready." She sensed his hand lifting in lazy farewell.

She looked at him and saw to her relief that he was wearing black swimming trunks. "I won't be long," she promised.

She let him get out of the house and then on impulse ran out on to the semicircular balcony. From this vantage point she saw him streaking down to the water's edge, a long, lean, bronzed flash of magnificent manhood.

She smiled, not totally in appreciation of his fine form. If she hadn't been here—with no one to witness his moonlight bathe, he wouldn't have bothered with the swimming trunks. He'd put them on as a sop to her prudery.

Some sop. As she watched he deftly removed the brief garment, flung it down on the moon-blanched sand, and raced into the sea, his powerful legs splashing up a waterfall before he dove, cleaving a path with his broad shoulders and muscular arms.

Her deep sigh was almost a mark of envy. It would be heavenly to do the same—shed her inhibitions with her swimsuit, float on the water, buoyant and free, supple and sinuous, with nothing to restrict her movements—no hampering straps cutting into her flesh, just the exhilarating feel of water against her skin.

Once started, her thoughts ran riot. She gazed up at the moon. It was enormous, languorous, drugging her senses, inveigling its way into her mind. She didn't try to resist. If the ocean in all its vastness was subservient to its dominance, what chance had she? Her eyes appealed to the half-naked marble nymph that had captured her heart this morning on her long walk around the veranda below. "You wouldn't be shocked, would you?"

She ran back into the bedroom, cast off the rest of her clothes, and dropped them on top of her swimsuit.

She was almost out of the house when she saw it, a splash of red and black on the tiled floor. She stopped—looked—struggling to work out the implication of finding it here with a mind that was still moon-drugged. She crouched down, bending over it, delaying the moment of picking it up, even in her moon-drugged state knowing that it would hurt her.

She came out of her stupor and scooped up the length of red-and-black material and held in her fingers the scarf David had worn for the barbecue. It told her

conclusively that this was where he had disappeared to
on the night of the barbecue when he'd been missing
for so long . . . when *they* had been missing. This was
where he'd brought Justine. He'd brought his mistress
here, tainting this perfect place with her presence. How
could he do this to her? She had been wrong in thinking
that making her dine with his mistress was the worst
possible act of cruelty—this was!

The treachery didn't stop there. She remembered
with stabbing clarity his familiarity with the house
knowing just where to put out his hand for the light
switches, making straight for the bedroom with an
unfaltering step. The night of the barbecue wasn't the
only time he'd been here with Justine. This was their
love nest.

This secret, hidden place where two people could lie
side by side, unobserved in sun worship, could swim in
the sea by the light of the moon, make love all night in
the wide double bed or pillowed on the white sand,
drowning in the bliss of this lovers' paradise, delighting
in each other. He must have found Justine the ideal
playmate. She had no inhibitions to shed. She wouldn't
have needed persuading not to wear a swimsuit before
going for a moonlight swim.

Oh, heavens . . . dear, merciful heavens . . . how
could he have done this to her?

Not that Justine didn't have a perfect right to come
here anytime she wished. It was her husband's house.
Petrina's agitated fingers clenched and unclenched. The
pain of her fingernails digging into the palms of her
hands, savaging the thin material of the scarf, was
nothing to the pain in her heart. The depth of her grief
scoured bitterness into her soul. Her cheeks flamed,
her eyes were wrathful as she vilified David for bringing

her on their so-called honeymoon to the house that belonged to the husband of his mistress.

This lovely house in this perfect setting . . . spoiled for her.

She rose to her feet with dignity, keeping her head high and a firm grip on the scarf. If she'd missed seeing it she would have gone out to David and afterward, their bodies relaxed and exhilarated by their swim, they would have made love. She looked at the scarf. It was lunacy to wish she hadn't seen it. Lunacy. That was it. She had looked too long at the moon. She was still under its influence. It was lunar madness to think there might be any explanation other than the one she had arrived at.

And yet . . . could her instincts have played her so false? This morning, on coming down to the bay, and more recently on entering the house, she'd felt a wonderful sense of belonging—of coming home. How could anything that had connections with Justine—or Geoffrey Hyland, for that matter—enfold her in homey warmth? It was just one more tragedy for her plagued mind to deal with.

She walked back into the bedroom, dragged her nightgown from her suitcase, and put it on. What else could she do? Home was too far away and too inaccessible. She looked at the bedroom door and saw the key in the lock. There was something she could do. She locked the bedroom door, returned and got into bed, but there was only anger in her heart and no sense of triumph.

She heard David come back. He shouted to her through the door, "So you changed your mind? Your loss, it was great. I won't be long; I'm just going to have a quick shower."

He didn't seem to notice that she hadn't replied. She heard the sound of the bathroom door opening, and the rush of running water. Soon . . .

When the door didn't yield, he rattled the knob. "What's the matter with the door?"

"It's locked."

"I see. Unlock it," he rapped out in command.

"No."

"I said . . . unlock it."

"I don't choose to."

"Please yourself. You open this door, or I smash it in."

"You wouldn't!"

"You have five seconds to weigh the odds."

He would!

She fumed at her own stupidity. What had possessed her to put herself in this position? Bad as it was, the consequence of not backing down was worse. She couldn't have Geoffrey Hyland sniggering at the implication of a broken door.

"One—two—"

"Yes, blast you!"

"—three—four—"

"I'm coming!"

"—fi—" Before the fifth second was completely counted out he was looking down at her flushed face, his eyes blazing, his lips bitten together in fury.

He seized her by the arms, which was perhaps as well because the grip that left her no room to maneuver concealed to some extent, but not altogether, the violence of her trembling.

"Calm down," he ordered, hardly helping matters by grinding the words out at her icily, his anger held back to a dangerous degree. "Don't ever try to bar me from your room—or your bed—ever again."

158

His pallor, beneath his tan, scared her breath into a frightening lump that she seemed unable to swallow round. In the temporary absence of coherent speech her eyes drove into his, twin missiles of smoky brown-violet condemnation, the gold irises, nature's precious and most eloquent gift, glittering in temper. "You . . . are . . . despicable."

"And you aren't making sense." His body towered over her, tense and savage, and there was something in his expression that seemed to be trying to understand.

He must have the hide of a rhinoceros, be totally lacking in finer feelings and the first elements of common decency, for not understanding, for looking at her as though she wasn't behaving in a perfectly reasonable manner.

"You've got a nerve," she screamed at him, "bringing me to this place."

"May the heavens grant me patience. I thought you'd like it here. I thought it would meet with your approval. I'm sorry it doesn't."

His mockery, his strained politeness, gave her the stamina to go on. "I approve of the place. It's enchanting. I love the house—its secluded position—the bay—everything! It's the human association I disapprove of—and that's putting it mildly—the human association that I hate. Now do you understand what I'm saying?"

"Oh, yes, now I understand. I apologize for being so slow. It must have been very trying for you." Below the arrogance of his eyes, his mouth was clamped in an expression of bitter acrimony through which his voice emerged, each syllable dropping like an icy spike into her brain. "It's finally made it through to me—you do hate me."

Chapter Ten

"Hate you?"

What did he mean? Being under the surveillance of his eyes, blue, with the sheen of ice chilling into her soul, was not designed to promote lucid thought. It was some moments before his words sank in, and it took longer to make sense of them. When she said it was not the house she hated but its human association, how could he think she meant him? She meant Justine, who was associated with the house through her husband's ownership of it.

Her thoughts split, so that while she was still basing most of her calculations on the belief that Geoffrey Hyland was the main power on the island and that the house belonged to him, an offshoot of thought brought to mind the suitcase David had brought with him, a suitcase which wasn't much larger than her own vanity case. He wouldn't need to bring much if he kept spares at the house, as he would if he owned it. It would also explain his ease of entry. He had walked in as though he were coming home . . . which was exactly what he had been doing. This was David's house.

How stupid of her not to have found the fault in her reasoning sooner. How could she have believed for one moment that someone of Geoffrey Hyland's evil character could possess the sensitive eye that had searched out this perfect spot, creating a sanctuary, a retreat of unsurpassed beauty and absolute tranquillity.

"Work on it," he cut in, his voice trailing sarcasm with every bitter note. "You're almost there."

Of course! The full implication hit her. If Geoffrey Hyland didn't own the house, it meant that he wasn't the brain behind the violation of her father's cherished dream.

Of their own compulsion, with no direction from her, the words exploded from her mouth. "You are the top man!" Every syllable rang with the long-stored hate she felt for the man behind the takeover venture, the man whose schemes had supplanted her father's own ambitions for Chimera.

"I knew you'd get there eventually. Yes, I am the major shareholder, the opportunist, the ruthless profiteer. You've hung so many titles around my neck that I don't know which one you prefer. Not that it matters—it all amounts to the same thing. I am the man—I've just thought of another title, one you openly regret—the man you vilify for cashing in on your father's dream is none other than your own beloved husband."

Even with his hair wildly undisciplined and glistening with droplets of water from his recent shower, and without clothes save for the bath sheet secured around his middle, he still had not divested himself of his mantle of authority. He would always stand like a king

161

among men. Proud, tall, no hint of apology or self-recrimination touching the perfect symmetry of his features, the strong chin, the noble and contemptuous curves of his mouth.

It was written in his expression that he had no intention of justifying his reasons for not telling her, and he was still actively censuring her attitude. His eyes reproved her for clinging to the dream and not accepting the reality. She'd lived with this way of thinking for too long to be able to drop it in an instant. It was unreasonable of him to expect it. And—she couldn't lose sight of this fact—it was her father's back he had climbed on. How could he stand before her so superior and scathing? Did he expect her to praise him for his achievement?

"Husband, yes. Leave out the beloved," she spat at him venomously.

At least, the words came from her lips, but they seemed to be speaking themselves. Her mind was stumbling through corridors of numbness, opening doors, seeking what? That streak of fairness that was not entirely dormant within her? She knew, although she didn't want to, had never wanted to, that there was much to praise in what he'd achieved. The people weren't exploited as she had first thought; they were sharing in the new prosperity. With the extra money in their pockets they were able to buy new, labor-saving devices to work their land. The expanding hotel complex—and others, some on the drawing board and some already in the advanced stages of construction on various parts of the island—provided a ready market for all they could produce, and at a fair price. Duplicates of the shawl David had given her this evening, its exquisite and distinctive pattern branding it the work of a Chimeran woman, could be seen in the local shops. The women were more eager to get out their crocheting hooks now that their sole outlet wasn't some unscrupulous exporter who was only prepared to give them a pittance for their hours of painstaking work.

She knew all this. She knew that the young people who had left the island and had been attracted back would stay. The old people would see their grandchildren grow up. Why couldn't she admit to him that her father's limited plan wouldn't have had such a widespread and beneficial effect?

His hard voice cut into her softening thoughts. "You're just like your father, clinging to an illusion."

That's why she couldn't unbend. Because of his superior attitude. It stuck in her throat and she refused to climb down. "Why didn't you tell me?" she demanded brokenly.

"Surely that's obvious?"

She stubbornly refused to admit to her bigoted attitude. "Not to me. You knew I thought you were carrying out someone else's orders."

"Yes, I knew."

"Why did you deceive me?"

"Ah, that's something I'm not guilty of."

His smile was cruel. Good. It hardened her own determination. "You're guilty by omission."

"That I cannot contradict. I was thinking of you there, believe it or not. I didn't think you were up to knowing. I thought that by the time you found out you would be better able to cope." His tone was touched with irony and he shrugged as though he should have known better. "I never deliberately set out to conceal the truth. If that had been my intention I would have brought you straight here. Instead, I took you to the

hotel where the evidence was all around for you to see.
I don't know why you didn't. It crossed my mind that
this could be in my favor. I thought that by the time it
did eventually click, you would have assessed things for
yourself and I might not seem the villain you thought I
was."

"You have an answer for everything, haven't you?"

He had been so unbelievably cool, setting the facts
before her with amazing self-control, that the sudden
heat in his voice took her by surprise. "Why don't you
open your tight little mind for once? If I hadn't cashed
in on your father's dream, as you've so often accused
me of doing, what do you think would have happened
to him?"

Refusing to be intimidated, she said, "You enjoy
being cruel, so I know you're going to tell me."

"It isn't something you don't already know. Your
father's position was critical. His financial affairs were
in such a mess he would have gone to jail."

"Thank you for reminding me. I might have forgotten."

"Be fair, Petrina. I'm not trying to deny the fact that
I've capitalized on his ideas, even those that failed."

"That's magnanimous of you."

"Will you close your prejudiced mouth and listen?
Without Benjamin Nightingale, all this wouldn't have
come about. The people here would still be breaking
their hearts and their backs trying to earn a living,
because all I did was expand on the original idea. There
was good in what your father set out to do, and if he'd
leveled down to practicalities instead of building on a
dream he would have succeeded. I saw the potential. If
I hadn't stepped in someone else would have, and your
father might not have had the fair deal I gave him."

"You'll be saying next that you did it all for my father and that lining your own pocket was a bonus!"

"I'd advise you not to strain my patience too far, Petrina."

The look on his face told her that it was good advice to take; her inner turmoil made it difficult to follow. She refrained from answering back, but not without effort.

Taking up from where he left off, he said, "Three years ago, at the time of your father's first financial crisis, I vowed to do three things. One was to pick Chimera up again, exploit your father's idea and *not* the people," he said pointedly.

Again she resisted the urge to speak.

"The second task I set myself was to recompense all the small investors who had lost their savings. I'm in the process of doing that now."

"You mean people my father cheated," she was stung to retort, unable to hold her silence a moment longer. "Why don't you say it? After all, it's what you're thinking."

"If you say so."

She sent him a withering look.

He combated it with a smile that had the distinction of curling his mouth up at the corners without the merit of warmth. "You have no cause to look affronted. You brought it on yourself. You goad me to say things I don't want to."

"*I* goad *you!*" she spluttered.

"At last we agree on something."

"We agree on nothing! If I were to listen to you, you'd have me believe that your motives throughout were based on totally unselfish reasons."

"You haven't let me finish, Pet," he said, deliberately sliding her name off his tongue in that cold mocking way that was such sensuous torture. "I haven't told you the third thing I vowed to do three years ago. That was strictly for me, and not even I can make it sound anything other than self-indulgent."

It didn't take much intelligence on her part to know the nature of his self-indulgence, not with the sensuous tone of his voice correlating with the sensuously assessing look in his eye to guide her. She returned his look with one of loathing.

He knew that what happened between them three years ago was something she would rather forget. No woman likes to be reminded of the time she threw herself at a man, blatantly letting him know that any thoughts he might have in her direction would not be repulsed—only to be repulsed herself. And that was what she had done. She had told David that she loved him and he had rebuffed her.

"I'm referring, of course, to that matter of unfinished business between us. I knew it couldn't be left like that and I promised myself that one day I'd come back and finish what you had started. I was tempted, you know, to finish it there and then."

Her head was flung back. "No, I didn't know."

"You were a provocative little peach. How I resisted tasting the fruit that was offered to me, I'll never know. Perhaps it was because I knew if I bit into it I would find that it was still green, better left on the tree to ripen."

She winced. "My father still needed me then, but you weren't thinking of him. You thought I'd be a pain in your stomach."

"Perhaps. I knew that one day I would come back for you."

All the time he'd stood aloof from her, mocking her, was it running through his mind to come back for her? Oh, no! She wasn't stupid enough to believe that. This was only another of his taunts.

"But why are we wasting time talking about it?" he said, a slight huskiness entering his voice. "This, after all, is the proper beginning of our honeymoon."

"You're not suggesting—" she began aghast.

His eyes narrowed. "I'm not suggesting anything. I'm telling you that this isn't going to be a repeat of the fiasco of our wedding night."

"No!" He couldn't be so cruel to her, demoralizing her in argument one moment and expecting to make love to her the next.

"Yes," he insisted with deadly emphasis.

"You once said you would never take an unwilling woman to bed."

"That still holds true. If it sounds like a reprieve, think again. It just means I'm going to have a lot of fun—and I promise that you will enjoy it too—in making you willing. This is the one area of our life that's right, and it's going to stay that way. We'll just have to argue out the other issues until you see reason."

His unbeatable arrogance, his audacity were unbelievable. She would never see his so-called reason. Agreed, their only common meeting ground was physical, but even that meeting was not achieved without conflict in her heart. Never once had he said "I love you." It would have made all the difference. He didn't love her, only her body. He only cherished it, lavished attention upon it to obtain for himself the utmost gratification. How degrading to know that his selfish caresses also gave her pleasure. *Had* given her pleasure, she amended silently. Now that she knew who he was, the major role he'd played in commercializing on her father's dream, she felt so cold toward him that she didn't think she would ever respond to him again.

She could almost laugh at his conceit in thinking that all he had to do was reach out to her, touch her, and she would melt against him. Tonight it would take more than even his special powers of persuasion to woo her past the chasm this disclosure had opened between them. *This* was the man she loved, the man who could do all this to her and still expect her sensual acquiescence. This man . . .

Although her father had lived for three years after his plans for Chimera had crashed in financial ruin, that, and not subsequent events, had been the reason he'd lost his will to live. Even if David had played no part in bringing her father down, he'd been quick to reach the scene to find out just what was in it for him.

"Profiteer. Opportunist. Vulture," she flung at him with such vehemence that she startled even herself.

Tears of cold exhaustion filled her eyes. She hid her face in her hands, shutting out the dark anger sweeping across his face. When she drew her hands away again, he had gone. She didn't know where he'd gone, and cared less. She dabbed her tears with her handkerchief, but when she looked at it she saw that it wasn't her handkerchief at all. The crumple of red and black twisting in her fingers was the scarf he'd worn for the barbecue, which she had found here. The issue of her father had completely taken over, blanking everything else out. She had forgotten to confront him with the scarf and tell him she knew he'd brought Justine here. She had forgotten that this sweet haven was *their* love nest. She didn't care about that anymore either. She didn't care about anything.

Her brain had taken one shock too many and had found its own way of dealing with the situation. It had shut off and was ready to sleep.

She opened her eyes to the morning with a dreadful weight on her heart. Memory lagged a step behind and she came through the moments of limbo between sleeping and being fully awake, wondering at the horrific nature of the dream responsible for her despair only to plunge even deeper into despair when she realized it wasn't a dream. It had happened. Her eyes flicked nervously across the bed, widening on the smoothness of the pillow and the unrumpled state of the sheets on that side.

If only some power had cut her impulsive tongue out of her head. She wished she could call back all those corrosive things she had said to him, things she hadn't meant anyway. She groaned aloud. She had been carried away by her own feelings to the point of being blind to the truth, deaf to the voices of reason crying out in her mind to be heard.

She dragged herself out of bed and crossed the room to open the heavy blinds and look out at the new day with reproving eyes. How could the sky be such a vivid blue and the sun be so bright while she was so unhappy?

Had David left her, she wondered, and gone back to the hotel? No, she couldn't hear him, but she could sense his electric presence, and besides, she had now identified the smell of freshly percolated coffee.

She showered, dressed, and made her way to the kitchen.

"The smell of coffee is better than an alarm clock," he said, filling a cup, picking it up by its saucer and handing it to her.

"Thank you." As she accepted it she anxiously searched his face for something in his expression to give her comfort. Nothing. His icy politeness amounted to indifference.

"Another beautiful day," he said in a tone better reserved for a casual acquaintance he didn't particularly wish to encourage. "You've missed the best part of it. I've been for a swim."

His attitude jarred. How she hated this smooth manner that could shake off last night's bitterness as if it had made no more impact than water on a seal's back. How dare he look so unruffled while she was quivering with fury and hurt? She set her cup and saucer down quickly before its rattle gave her away.

What good would having yesterday back do for her? She had blamed her own deficiencies, her blind loyalty to her father and her intolerance of any plans David had for Chimera that did not exactly follow the original format. She had forgotten how exasperating he could be when he set his mind to it. There was also the matter of the scarf, which hadn't been sorted out yet. Given yesterday back, she would behave in just the same way.

"Hungry?" he inquired.

"Starving," she said. She would beat him at his own game by not admitting to her loss of appetite in case he remembered—and he would—her inability to eat well when she was unhappy or in a temper. She would eat with gusto even if it choked her. She would not give him the satisfaction of knowing that even for a moment she had regretted her part in what had happened between them last night.

"By a strange coincidence, I anticipated you would

be—" Blast his sneering mouth and his shrewd, knowing eyes! "—so I took the things out of the fridge for a full English breakfast. I've done my share, now it's your turn. I like my bacon crispy."

He folded his arms and tipped his chair back on two legs, in line with the angle of his head. Was he going to sit there and watch her?

"Is there a clean tea cloth or something I could wrap around me to protect my dress, please?"

"I'm pretty certain that Carmen keeps a spare apron somewhere. But as any apron that accommodates her splendid hips will wrap around you three times, perhaps you'd better settle for the tea cloth. There's one on the rail."

"Carmen?" she queried, reaching for the linen cloth and fastening it around her waist before taking up her station by the stove.

"The woman who keeps an eye on the house for me. Cleans, stocks up the fridge—all that."

Ah, yes! The *señora* she'd talked to on discovering the bay.

"She was here bright and early this morning with our daily bread, and she's coming back later in time to cook our supper. I told her to leave the cleaning and that we'd forage lunch for ourselves."

She had spotted the selection of crusty and soft rolls and the loaf of bread and wondered where they'd come from. "Sounds fine to me," she said in an offhand voice, layering strips of bacon across the frying pan.

Had things been right between them it would have been more than fine. It would have been idyllic to be alone here with her husband, cooking for him, cleaning. In kinder circumstances she would have been tempted to ask him to send Carmen away so she could cook the evening meal as well. But . . .

His hard voice crushed into her thoughts. "You don't have to look so dismayed. I'm not condemning you to a day of domestic chores. The house won't fall down if it misses getting the flick of a duster and fruit and rolls will suffice for lunch."

"I'm glad to hear it," she said, transferring the bacon onto a plate and cracking the eggs into the frying pan.

"I can see why," he said drily.

She looked down into the frying pan and saw that out of the three eggs, two of the yolks were broken. He'd put her off by sitting there in high and mighty anticipation of a ruined breakfast. Knowing that while she was useless in lots of things, cooking was a natural asset—something she loved doing and did well—added to her frustration.

"There," she said slamming the plate down on the table in front of him. Her expression clearly said, "I hope it chokes you." She set the basket of rolls on the table and went back for her own plate.

They lay side by side on the warm sand, close, yet apart. Since breakfast, they had hardly spoken.

He emerged from a deep, pensive silence to say, "It can't go on like this."

"No," she agreed. "What do you intend to do about it? It's obvious you've given it some thought."

"Yes, I have." He was lying on his front, wearing the black swimming trunks he'd discarded before going for his swim last night. He levered himself up on his elbows and looked at her. The burning sun that was baking her skin a deeper shade of golden brown was not as fierce as the torrid torture of the all-over exploration his eyes were making of her body. His scrutiny made her perspire; moisture beaded her upper lip and the hollow

172

between her breasts left exposed by the cut of her swimsuit. "I'm sending you home," he said starkly.

How could he look at her in that ravishing, hungry way and placidly announce that he was sending her home? Her mouth rounded on a small, hysterical laugh: "Home? You mean home to England?"

"My timing was off, Pet," he said in dry self-derision. "I came back for you too soon. You were only a woman on the outside. Inside, you were still an adolescent with your head full of dreams."

Last night she would have given anything to be home. Now she didn't want to go. She closed her eyes against the expression on his face and the vivid blue, sheet-of-glass look of the sky. The dazzle remained under her eyelids as tears she must not let him see.

"I'm not an adolescent," she said. "You'll have to come up with a better explanation than that."

"I don't have to explain anything," he said in quiet menace, "but I will. I've a job to do. I can't give it my best while you're around. I've tried to be patient with you, but I've finally had to admit that it's not going to work. Your prejudices go too deep and I just can't deal with the situation. It will be better for both of us if you go home."

His work—that's all he cared about. He wasn't a man running on normal feelings; he was a robot powered on ambition. That hard streak of ruthless dedication hadn't taken long in coming through.

"Look," he said swiftly, "I know it sounds as if I'm putting the onus on you, but I'm not. I'm to blame. I should have known my workload was too heavy to accommodate a bride. Brides should be spoiled a little, be given time and attention. It's their right. I should have known you'd be too much of a distracting influence to have around."

"I don't know how you have the nerve! I haven't managed to distract you from Justine. When you both disappeared from the barbecue I know you came here," she blurted out hotly, "because I found the scarf you'd been wearing and it didn't walk here by itself."

"No. It's true that I left the barbecue to come here. The storm was about to break. I wondered if Carmen had remembered to make sure the shutters were secure. I decided to check for myself rather than risk bringing you here and finding the place half wrecked."

"Oh! But Justine came with you?" she persisted.

"I see now what last night's lockout was about," he said, a mocking smile on his mouth. "If you've made up your inexorable little mind that I brought Justine here, nothing I say will convince you to the contrary."

"How can I believe there's nothing going on between you and Justine when you won't give me a straight answer? You despise Geoffrey Hyland as much as I do. You wouldn't have anything to do with him if Justine weren't involved. You tolerate him to be near her."

"Hasn't it occurred to you there might be another consideration? I could be tolerating his money. If he hadn't come in with me, I couldn't have taken up the option on Chimera. You didn't think I had access to that much ready cash myself, did you?"

"I never gave that side of it a thought." She wasn't too forgiving. He hadn't denied involvement with Justine, only admitted to *another* consideration. She kept the thought that it couldn't have been easy for him to include a man like that in the deal sealed behind her lips.

"I had it written into the contract that I could buy him out."

"That's something, anyway."

"He had the foresight to insert a time clause."

Which explained why he had been working himself into the ground. "Can you beat it?"

"I must." His mouth hardened. "I won't let anything, or anyone, stop me."

Meaning me, she thought. "David, this is going to sound terribly repetitive. I'm tired of saying 'Why didn't you tell me?' But why *didn't* you tell me about the time clause?" She couldn't bear the thought that her presence, her behavior, might stop him from beating Geoffrey Hyland. If she'd known she wouldn't have been so obstructive.

"Perhaps I thought it was in my own best interest not to tell you. If you'd known that, you might have been even more demanding of my time. Anything to prevent my getting sole control of your precious Chimera."

She bit her lip, disturbed and shaken. Then anger came to cancel out all other emotions. Anger against herself for softening toward him. If he could think that of her, let him. "How well you know me," she said haughtily.

She placed her hands on the beach towel she was lying on, swinging her feet around and under her. His hand came out and held her in this half-rising position. "Where do you think you're going?"

"In the house to shower and dress. Then you can take me back to the hotel. If your mind is made up, I see no point in delaying. We might as well get back so that you can arrange my flight home as soon as possible."

"No. We came here for two weeks. That's how long we're staying."

She tried to find a reason for his decision not to send her home straight away. She had a horrible suspicion that she was going to regret this in a moment, but could it be that he wasn't going to send her home? Was it a bluff? Had he said he was sending her home with no serious intention of carrying out this threat—to shock her into seeing reason? Or had he meant it then but regretted it now, and was he playing for time in the hope that two weeks on their own would work its own magic and the situation would come right between them?

His derisive, scorn-flecked eyes held hers. "You don't think I'm going to let you make a laughingstock of me by returning to the hotel after only one day of our official honeymoon, do you?"

She should have known better. "You'd make me stay here against my will to save your face?" she said contemptuously.

"Against your will?" The hand that had stopped her from getting up slid into the deep cutaway side of her swimsuit, seeking its own answer.

He angered and irritated her to the point of screaming frustration. His mocking tongue violated her sensitivity and pride. What pride? Her pride was useless when compared with the effect his strong fingers had on her senses.

His hand moved around to her front, teased over her already tautened stomach muscles, hesitated deliberately so that her body didn't know which part of it was going to delight to his touch. He kept her there, suspended on intolerable expectation, his fingers moving tormentingly backward and forward across her stomach.

"The sun is very hot. Your skin is burning. Shall we go in? If you stay out much longer you'll pay the consequences," he said.

The better part of the day lay ahead of them, with no fear of interruption until Carmen came to start the evening meal. If she went inside with him she would pay another kind of consequence.

His fingers applied themselves to a more penetrating exploration. His hand moved slowly under her suit top to cup her breast, teasing the nipple until it tautened to his touch. She knew he was testing her. Afterward she would remind herself of this and console herself with the fact that she had tried to act upon the knowledge by endeavoring to cool her emotions. Now his mouth as well as his hands was pursuing her. She turned agonizingly away from his lips, but he anticipated she would do this and his chin swerved faster than hers, cutting off escape and deflecting her mouth into the kiss.

It was too much. Suddenly she was pouring all the sweet selflessness of her love into the kiss she gave him back. He paused in what he was doing, even his lips held still in surprise. Then his mouth took the initiative once more, closing against hers in a kiss of brutal passion; at the same time his hands no longer delicately pampered but took bitter delight in revenging themselves on her body. It was as if he was punishing her for some misdeed she was not aware of committing.

Her brain went into shock at the unexpectedness of it, though the blockage to her mind wasn't total because she still had a thread of reasoning faculty. She knew he was hurting her deliberately. Why? And yet still he was giving her pleasure. How could she enjoy his cruel passion?

Her mind objected strongly, but her body was on a different level and it shamed her with its fevered response. She could not understand the twisted state of her emotions that made her react this way.

The abuse stopped. His hands no longer pursued her and her body stopped burning to the abrasive roughness of his caresses, leaving her feeling strangely bereft.

Perhaps she had become acquiescent because she sensed something out of the ordinary, a reason she was slow to comprehend. Her gentle lover hadn't turned into her tormentor without just cause.

She looked at him through her lashes and saw his suffering, the pain and torment of barely controlled passion. She raised up her body, touched his cheek in a gesture of understanding and compassion, and knew she was looking into the face of self-denial. Why?

A muscle jumped under her fingertips before her hand was dragged savagely away. She couldn't understand the dark anger in his eyes. "So that's how it is. You'd do anything to tie my hands so I can't do any more harm to your precious Chimera. I can violate your body, but my hands must be kept off Chimera. It's too late. Progress won't stop if I don't regain full control. The plans are too far advanced. But perhaps that no longer matters. What *is* important to you is that *I* don't gain control."

"David, I honestly don't know what you're talking about."

"You she-devil. You've never been like this before . . . all sweetness and fire. I can do what I like with you and you won't stop me. You'll even encourage me to do more."

"I'm your wife. Please—you're not making sense."

"Don't lie to me. One thing I've always admired in you is the honest way you defend your ideals. Your unbending attitude to the changed face of the island has always angered me, but never before have you hidden behind pretense. I've argued with you about it, but I've admired the way you've upheld your viewpoint with honesty and courage. I don't like this turnabout. I don't admire you for what you'd be willing to do to thwart me. I made a big mistake in telling you I can't do my job properly when you're around because I find you too much distraction. You're using it as a weapon against me. You think if I make love to you for two weeks, I won't be able to send you away—and you're right. If you stayed, I could never beat the time clause. So I cannot allow you to stay."

She shook her head in stunned disbelief. Did he really think she was vindictive enough to do that to him? Why was she so surprised at his opinion? She'd tried to block him all the way, scornful of what he'd achieved, making dreadful accusations. He didn't even know that he'd won her around to his way of thinking because she'd been too stubborn to tell him.

She tried to tell him now. "I've been wrong, David. I want you to beat the time clause. I can't bear the thought of your being bound to a man like Geoffrey Hyland. I'll do anything. I won't distract you. I'll keep out of the way."

He listened to her in silence, a mirthless smile on his lips, and then he said harshly, "No, Petrina. We must endure one another's company. I can see no way around that because I will not humiliate myself by returning to the hotel until a decent interval has elapsed, although it doesn't have to be dragged out for the full fortnight. Meanwhile, you won't distract me for the simple reason that I won't let you. I intend to keep out of *your* way as much as possible."

She realized wearily that he thought this was another trick to make him lose his head. Some hope of that. She looked deep into his eyes, glinting at her in anger, and saw no affection, no tenderness on his face. Her heart lurched in despair as she acknowledged to herself the futility of trying to make him see.

The roles were reversed. How ironic that just when she had come to believe in him, to trust him, he was suspicious and distrustful of her.

The days weren't so bad. She could stretch out on her solitary towel on the white sand and let the sun dull her senses. The nights, spent alone in the vast double bed, were more difficult to bear.

The situation could not be hidden from Carmen, who came in daily to bring supplies and to clean and cook for them. She knew they slept in separate bedrooms and was clearly puzzled by it. Her beloved *señor,* who had brought such happiness and prosperity to the island, could do no wrong in her eyes and so it was Petrina who was subjected to her reproachful glances.

After ten days of strained disharmony, David said they could return to the hotel. She heard him with a surge of relief. She couldn't have borne much more of this persecution, yet she dreaded the prospect of returning to the hotel with him, of being forced to return to England.

"David?" she asked in sudden inspiration, "do I have to come with you? Couldn't I stay here until you've arranged my flight home?"

"I can see no objection to that," he said, much to her surprise. "I'm sure Carmen will agree to remain at night instead of returning to her own home."

"That won't be neccessary. I shall be perfectly all right on my own."

"I disagree. In fact I must make it a stipulation. Until it's connected by telephone, this place is far too remote for me to consider leaving you here on your own. You would be too out of reach of help if, for example, you fell ill.''

Did he realize what he'd said? "Until it's connected by telephone"—implying that when it was he would allow her to stay here by herself. The situation had a less finite sound to it and she couldn't keep the sudden hope out of her eyes.

It struck him at the same time. "I know. It's hopeless," he said harshly. "I've worked harder on this project than on anything I've ever done in my life. I can't let it go now. But I can't let you go either. I want you both. If it's down to a choice"— he shrugged— "there's no contest, because I've got to have you.''

Had she heard right? For a moment, flinching at the savagery of his tone, she couldn't believe that such a humble admission could have come from this haughty mouth. Words such as those should be spoken in humility, not tossed out in arrogance. Did it matter? All that mattered was that he had spoken them and he wasn't going to send her away.

"Why can't you have both? I've changed, David, you must believe me. I mean to help now, not hinder. I've spoken impulsively, before I've understood. I've behaved like a woolly-minded contrary little girl and I don't know how you've stood me.''

"No tricks? You're on the level?" Although his tone was still skeptical and searching, she knew he was more than half way to believing her.

"I'm speaking the truth, David. I've been so wrong about you.''

"Thank heaven," he said, swallowing deeply. "It seems I could have been wrong about you too.''

His arms reached out for her and bound her to him in a fierce hug of silent homage. Her own throat was doing a lot of churning as she too gave prayerful thanks. It was going to be all right. David wasn't going to send her away, now or ever. After the way she had behaved, it was more than she deserved.

"Tears?" he said, tilting her chin.

"It's seemed so long and it's been so awful. I thought I was never going to get through to you. I feel so ashamed of how I was before. I set out to be as unreasonable as I could possibly be."

"Now don't go taking all the blame. I don't have a lot to be proud of myself. Going back to our wedding— that wasn't half the wedding you deserved. You even had to pick out your own wedding bouquet."

"I did it on impulse and then regretted it when I saw you were laughing at me."

He looked at her for a long moment. There was a fight going on behind his eyes. The decision to speak up was reached after deep self-searching, and the reluctance in his voice showed he was not certain he was doing the right thing. "I've a feeling I shouldn't be telling you this—it leaves me wide open—but I assure you I wasn't laughing at you."

"No?"

"Want proof?" She didn't know what he could mean and watched closely as he extracted a piece of tissue paper from his wallet. Unfolding it for her inspection, he said, "That's pretty substantial evidence, wouldn't you say?"

She was looking at a pressed wild rose—the dog rose she'd picked for his buttonhole that she thought he'd thrown away in scorn. He'd kept it and all this time he had been carrying it close to his heart. It certainly proved he hadn't been laughing at her, but that was a secondary consideration in the light of a possible new disclosure.

"You've got it," he said, as he read the bewildered

wonder on her face. "You know it all now, don't you? You know the other reason, besides my desire to make love to you, why I married you—if I'm truthful, the *only* reason I married you."

Her voice was anxious. It would be too painful if she'd tricked herself into believing something that wasn't true simply because she wanted to believe it so much. "You said that if ever there came a time when you felt inclined to tell me, it would be unnecessary because it would mean that I knew. I think I know, but I can't be sure." And then, overwhelmed at how close they had come to ruining it all, she said, "Oh, David, if you had sent me home, I think I would have died. And, anyway, it wouldn't have been home, because home is where you are."

"The same goes for me," he said gruffly. "We've both suffered, it seems."

"I'm still suffering. Tell me, David. Say it, *please*," she begged, running her hand down the hard lines of his face, sensing the softening of his expression with her fingertips as well as seeing it with her eyes.

"You stubborn, adorable woman, I love you. I seem to have loved you forever."

Was it possible, she wondered, to die of happiness? "There's something else I must ask you, and I promise never to mention it again. You and Justine . . . was there really nothing going on between you?"

"Geoff leaves her on her own too much. She can be good company. And I suppose I felt sorry for her for having Geoff for a husband. Does that answer your question?"

"Not altogether. You haven't said . . . that is . . . did you fancy her?"

"Come on, now," he mocked in the old dreaded way. "A man gets lonely and Justine's an attractive woman."

Her heart dropped and then he relented. "I've sacrificed everything for Chimera. Do you think I'd put it all in jeopardy by having an affair with Justine Hyland of all people? Use your common sense. Despite the fact that she and her husband go their separate ways in many things, she's still in the enemy camp. Convinced?" His voice dropped in bitter self-derision. "Justine, or any woman for that matter, would have had a hard time getting you out of my blood. I was telling the truth when I said I always knew that one day I'd come back for you. I never completely lost touch with what you were doing, thanks to my father. His letters always contained some piece of information about you. You didn't know I was keeping tabs on you, did you?"

"I'd no idea. Good thing I behaved myself." The words were impish, but the tone of her voice, low and husky, was still wondrously giving thanks.

"Mm." His eyebrow lifted. "You know as well as I do that my father would never have written anything to your discredit. I must invite him to come and visit us, as soon as I can bring myself to share you. He's always thought a lot of you. In his eyes, marrying you was my biggest triumph to date."

"Only in *his* eyes?" she couldn't resist asking.

"No, in mine as well. I've admitted so much—I might as well tell you everything. The things I'm striving for—all I've achieved—success would be hollow if you weren't by my side to share it with me. These past ten days I've been suffering the tortures of the damned. Finally bringing you here to *your* house—you must know it was built with you in mind—being on our own, wanting you with a driven, desperate hunger, and unable to touch you without making you hate me more than I thought you already did. I thought I would go crazy. It got to the point where I couldn't trust myself to be alone with you for another moment. The last time I touched you I was so rough with you, and I was sorry straight away. I vowed it would never happen again. But the strain of not touching you got worse each day, and I knew that I had to get back to the hotel before I did something really regrettable, something you couldn't possibly forgive. I'm not taking too much for granted, am I, in thinking you've forgiven me for the other?"

"Of course not. It was nothing. I'm not letting you go back to the hotel on your own now. I'm coming with you," she said fiercely.

"The situation's changed. We're not going, not yet anyway. It will be back to the grindstone soon enough." His eyes searched her face as if for confirmation. "No problem there—now that you're with me."

The fact that he was still not one hundred percent certain of her twisted her heart. All the time she had been accusing him of treating her so badly, what had she been doing to him?

"Oh, David, I love you so. I'm with you all the way."

"That will make all the difference. I'll be able to work twice as hard now that I know it's for both of us."

His hands went to her waist; hers lifted and wound around his neck where finger linked with finger to form a ring.

The sparkle came back to his eye to delight and torment her. "That little piece of seduction is what started it all. You did that, and I wanted to make love to you. Nothing's changed in that respect, except that perhaps the urge is even greater now. Ten days wasted out of fourteen." His groan turned into a growl of pleasure that flicked her senses into urgent response. "That's fourteen days of loving to cram into the four days we've got left."

His mouth lowered to hers. Without breaking the kiss—a kiss so deep and draining it was almost a fulfillment in itself—he lifted her up against his chest and carried her into the bedroom. He set her on the big bed where, together at last, they gave themselves over to the loving enjoyment of each other that they had so long been denied. He took his time, divesting her of each article of clothing with maddening slowness, refusing to let her respond in kind as his eyes and hands and lips took their fill of her. When she could wait no longer she wove her hands into the crisp thickness of his hair and pulled his mouth to hers. Her hands roved over his muscular body, seeking to give him the same pleasure he had brought her and removing all barriers to her full enjoyment of him.

With a groan of pleasure he gathered her tightly into his arms and, as the shadows lengthened in the room, told her without words what it meant to him to have her as his wife.

Epilogue

It was evening, Petrina's favorite time of day because David would soon be with her. The installation of a telephone might have stolen that feeling of total isolation they had once known, but this vital link had enabled them to make their home in her beloved Serpent's Tail Bay.

At first, David had often worked late into the evening, too, but the pressure had eased considerably since beating the time clause and she could count on his returning home at a reasonable time. The day he bought Geoffrey Hyland out of the contract had been memorable. She had let him wallow in his well-earned moment of triumph and then she had smugly informed him that they had a little something else to celebrate as well.

She hadn't thought it possible for anyone to know this much happiness. She would never take it for granted. Each day she took pride and joy in counting her blessings. Top of her list was having David for a husband; second, that their first child was on the way; and third came Chimera's continued prosperity, secure in David's capable and caring hands. When she looked around and saw all the good he was doing, she wondered how she could have been against him for so long.

Her attitude toward the future was realistic. She knew that when David had done all he could here, his brilliant brain would want to sharpen itself on a new challenge, which might take them away from Chimera. She would be sorry because she loved this sun-kissed island. But she loved David more. She could never envisage a time when they would stay away for good. Chimera had too strong a hold on their emotions not to bring them back, no matter how far or how many times David's work took them away. Chimera would always be here; built on a rock, it would remain forever as something solid in their lives to come back to.

Her ears alerted her to the sound of David's car. She was on her feet and running to meet him. Moments later she was where she most wanted to be—in his arms.

Silhouette Romance

THE NEW NAME IN LOVE STORIES

Six new titles every month bring you the best in romance.
Set all over the world, exciting and brand new stories about
people falling in love:

Silhouette Romance

THE NEW NAME IN LOVE STORIES

Silhouette Romance

THE NEW NAME IN LOVE STORIES

All these books are available at your local bookshop or newsagent, or can be ordered direct from the publisher. Just tick the titles you want and fill in the form below.

Prices and availability subject to change without notice.

SILHOUETTE BOOKS, P.O. Box 11, Falmouth, Cornwall.

Please send cheque or postal order, and allow the following for postage and packing:

U.K. — 40p for one book, plus 18p for the second book, and 13p for each additional book ordered, up to £1.49 maximum.

B.F.P.O. and EIRE — 40p for the first book, 18p for the second book, and 13p per copy for the next 7 books, 7p per book thereafter.

OTHER OVERSEAS CUSTOMERS — 60p for the first book plus 18p per copy for each additional book.

Name ....

Address...

....

Silhouette Romance

EXCITING MEN,
EXCITING PLACES, HAPPY ENDINGS . . .

Contemporary romances for today's women

If there's room in your life for a little more romance,
SILHOUETTE ROMANCES are for you.

And you won't want to miss a single one so start
your collection now.

Each month, six very special love stories will be yours
from SILHOUETTE.

Look for them wherever books are sold
or order from the coupon below.

No. 58 JOURNEY TO QUIET WATERS
     Dixie Browning   65p 27113 2
No. 60 GREEN PARADISE Heather Hill   65p 27115 9
No. 61 WHISPER MY NAME Fern Michaels   65p 27116 7
No. 62 STAND-IN BRIDE Carole Halston   65p 27117 5
No. 63 SNOWFLAKES IN THE SUN Audrey Brent 65p 27118 3

*All these books are available at your local bookshop or
newsagent, or can be ordered direct from the publisher. Just
tick the titles you want and fill in the form below.*

Prices and availability subject to change without notice.

SILHOUETTE BOOKS, P.O. Box 11, Falmouth, Cornwall.

Please send cheque or postal order, and allow the following for
postage and packing:

U.K. — 40p for one book, plus 18p for the second book, and
13p for each additional book ordered, up to £1.49 maximum.

B.F.P.O. and EIRE — 40p for the first book, 18p for the
second book, and 13p per copy for the next 7 books, 7p per
book thereafter.

OTHER OVERSEAS CUSTOMERS — 60p for the first book
plus 18p per copy for each additional book.

Name ....

Address...

....